Sinners Ride

Brandon Barrows

Sinners Ride

Full Speed Publishing

Table of Contents

Bonus Stories

It's a long, dusty road…

CHAPTER ONE

They strung him from a cottonwood tree that had seen better days. Its bark was split and curling like old paper left too long in the sun. Its limbs were bare in places where wind and drought had scoured them clean—but for all that, those limbs were strong. Sturdy enough to hold a man's weight.

The horizon burned gold behind a distant ridge, smearing the sky with rust and ash. It was hot, without even a hint of breeze. The air smelled of dust and sweat, closing in tight around a half-circle of horses and men clustered beneath the cottonwood. At their center, one man knelt in the dust, hands bound behind him, hat long gone, blood on his lips and drying on his chin.

"It was fair shootin'," Ben Keelock said through cracked teeth.

A fist answered him, fast and hard and unexpected, with a meat-and-gristle crack that knocked him backwards, off his knees, to sprawl in the dirt.

"Bullshit." It was snarled, the voice low and mean and carrying an unreasoning kind of resentment.

Keelock rolled in the dirt, blinked sweat and a fresh trickle of blood from his eyes, and looked up through a haze. A big man with walrus mustaches stood over him, rubbing his knuckles and glaring hatred Keelock had only rarely seen—and never before directed at him. The man was about fifty, getting heavy in the belly, but still powerful through the shoulders.

"Jay Cooley was the fastest draw I ever knew," the man growled. "Only way some saddle-bum drifter could kill him was a backshot."

Keelock spat blood into the dirt and met the man's glaring eyes. "Your friend was a liar and a trouble-hunter," he said. "He just found what he was lookin' for, and however it looks, it was fair shootin'."

The mustached man lunged, fists raised, fury all over his face, but two of the posse held him back, one to an arm, pulling him away from Keelock before he could throw another punch. One of the two, younger than the rest of the crowd, said, "Enough, Mister Brewster."

Keelock's gaze shifted to the youngster. Nelson, he heard one of the men call him earlier. He was twenty, maybe twenty-one, tanned and sweaty like the rest of the riders, but not yet hardened. He met Keelock's eyes for an instant before looking away—long enough for Keelock to see that he was troubled by all this, regretting his part in it.

You ain't the only one, Keelock thought bitterly.

Brewster twisted, straining against the others' grip, but the fight, the hatred, was already seeping out of him. His fists unclenched and some of the tension went out of his shoulders before he visibly sagged. He took another step back of his own accord and the two released him.

Nelson watched Brewster a moment, wary of any trickery, before shifting to Keelock. Keelock thought the boy looked as if wanted to believe him about the shooting, that Cooley started it, but he didn't have any room or reason for hope. Even if the youth believed him, there were five others who didn't, and he couldn't ask a kid to fight his battles.

"Makin' this uglier than it needs to be ain't bringin' Cooley back, Mr. Brewster," Nelson said.

The men around him nodded and muttered. No one looked pleased by any of this—the day had been ugly enough.

"Let's just get this over with," the young man said, already turning away.

Brewster's lip curled beneath the mustache. "You're right, son," he said, stepping back with a huff. "This is about justice, after all." He grinned and added, with a look that made the skin try to crawl off Keelock's spine, "String him up, boys."

Keelock's own horse had already been led

beneath the cottonwood, and the noose was ready, one end looped over a branch and the other tied tight around the cottonwood's trunk. Under Brewster's watch, Nelson and three others lifted Keelock to his feet and then took him by the arms and pushed him awkwardly up into the saddle. Keelock didn't struggle. He didn't beg. He had made his case and nobody listened, except maybe the boy, Nelson, and he didn't matter. Not now. Keelock sat straight in the saddle as the noose was thrown over his head and then tightened around his throat.

"Any last words?" Brewster asked, still grinning.

"Believe what you want." Keelock didn't raise his voice, and there was no anger in the words, only resignation and maybe a note of pity. "You're murderin' an innocent man. If there's any justice in this world, sooner or later you'll get yours."

Brewster sighed, slow and theatrical, shaking his head and lifting his shoulders in a shrug of feigned helplessness. "Do it."

Everything went still. The men clustered around the cottonwood hesitated. They weren't killers. Not really. And this had gone on too long—there'd been too much talk and lynching isn't any fun if it takes too long. It gave a man time to reflect and nobody wanted that. Nobody wanted to think about what they were doing. Jay Cooley was a bully and a braggart. Nobody much liked him, but he was a townsmen to all of them and now he was lying dead on a plank, and this drifter, Keelock, didn't deny shooting him. Keelock talked of justice, but eye for an eye was the only kind of justice they knew.

"I said do it!" Brewster barked.

The flat of a palm came down hard on the horse's flank. The horse reared and bolted, dust exploding beneath its hooves as the rope snapped taut with a brutal jerk. The world leapt, shifting out of focus, and then shattering into pieces as Keelock's boots kicked once, twice. His eyes bulged and a choked sound scraped its way from somewhere deep in his throat.

The wind came out of nowhere, stirring the cottonwood leaves. The wind and rapidly fading hoofbeats of Keelock's horse were the only sounds.

"We're done here, boys," Brewster said, throwing a leg over his saddle. He tugged at the reins and turned his mount towards home.

No one else spoke and no one moved for long moments, then a man in blue plaid removed his hat, lowered his head and muttered what might have been a prayer. Then, one by one, the men mounted and rode off without further ceremony, each on his lonesome, now just silhouettes in the gathering dusk to one another.

Nelson was the last man standing beneath the old cottonwood. He stared towards the horizon where the sun was fast fading, then climbed into his saddle and turned the horse towards town. He took a final look at the man hanging from the cottonwood.

"Sorry, mister," he whispered, scarcely audible over the creak and jangle of his saddle as he rode off.

CHAPTER
TWO

Ben Keelock swayed in the noose. His vision darkened and blood thundered in his ears like a thousand racing hooves pounding hardpan, but he heard the boy—just barely. Pain lanced his spine, shooting from his neck and spreading through his body. He wanted to cry out, to ask for help, but his only sound was a soft gurgling. He saw the guilt in the boy's face before and knew that away from the others, Nelson could be pushed to act. But the world was blurred with a red haze and Keelock's brain was slipping down a long, dark shaft. His legs twitched, then stilled as blackness closed around him.

Silence settled across the plain, thick and deep enough to drown in.

A voice, low and soft and indefinably not-quite-human, whispered out of the gathering hush. "Have they gone?"

Keelock's painfully bulging eyes somehow saw the soundless presence emerging from the brush clustered near the cottonwood: a coyote, its golden eyes catching what little light remained. Its manner was relaxed, unconcerned, its tongue lolling and its gait almost a saunter as it moved directly beneath the hanging man and looked upwards. Keelock was barely aware of the creature and yet his dimming brain could still tell that it was wrong in some way, like a dream pretending to be living flesh.

"Hello, Mister Keelock," it said without moving its mouth. "May I call you Ben?"

Keelock closed his eyes, his teeth clenching in agony as sweat poured down his face, and his first clear thought in some time came: Losing my mind.

"You're not," the coyote said, "but you are running out of time, so I'll cut to the chase."

The creature circled beneath him with the casual interest of a scavenger, its nose twitching, its eyes glinting, its tail swaying slowly side to side. It didn't pace so much as drift as it moved a few feet away, putting itself where Keelock could see it clearly. Its mouth curled in what almost looked like a smirk. It had too many teeth and its gaze was too knowing.

"You need a miracle, and I need a favor, Ben. Shall we help each other?"

Keelock's heart pounded once then stuttered as his vision tunneled. The world around him peeled away like corn shuck, and then the darkness closed in again as everything disappeared into flecks of black and red. Everything but the coyote—sitting before him, composed, ears perked and patient, as polite as you could ask for. Keelock opened his mouth, but nothing came out—no words, not even a gasp of breath.

"No need to strain yourself," the coyote said. "A thought will suffice. Better hurry, though."

Just let me breathe! Keelock's mind screamed.

Blackness came crashing—not falling, but snapping like a trap slamming shut—and even the coyote disappeared.

Keelock stared up into a sky so blue it stung. His breath came in hot rasps as he blinked, squinting into glaring sunlight, watching shreds of clouds moving dizzy-fast across the heavens, like white-water racing down a flooded river.

He lay flat on his back, aware now of the uneven ground, of rocks digging into his flesh, and of the dry wind blowing across his face. He sat up slowly, every joint aching. Dried blood flaked from his chin as he rubbed both hands across his face. "What the hell?" he groaned. "Some kinda loco dream?"

His fingers found the raw grooves circling his neck. The skin was welted and hot to the touch, abraded deep enough to sting in the dry air, and his neck swollen so that swallowing felt like he had a throat full of razors.

Keelock groaned again. "No damned dream ever chafed like this."

A whinny cut the silence. Nearby a tall, chestnut mare stood motionless. Even in the thin flat light of the open plain, her coat shone like burnished copper and her black mane hung in thick waves. She was saddled and waiting, watching Keelock inquisitively. Her reins hung loose, and resting on the saddle horn was a hat—his hat, weathered and sweat-stained and familiar.

"Well, hello, pretty lady," Keelock said, hauling himself to his feet and approaching the horse. She moved to meet him, eyes flicking, and wickering in greeting. She nuzzled him eagerly, her nose against his shoulder, as if she already knew him and had been waiting a long time for his return.

"Where'd you come from?" he murmured, running a hand along her sleek flank. The horse was all muscle and sinew and warmth, solid beneath his touch, but his fingers paused at the brand burned into her hide: a stylized coyote's head, wide-mouthed and grinning.

Keelock snorted. "Guess that shouldn't be no surprise, huh?"

He swung up into the saddle, marveling at the feel, at how it conformed to his backside as if it had always belonged to him. "Well, dream or not, you're the best-looking piece of horseflesh I've ever seen, girl. And I never could resist a fine horse, nor a fine lady, neither." The horse whinnied as if acknowledging the compliment.

Keelock set his hat on his head, adjusted the fit, and then touched his heels lightly to the mare's sides, sending her moving at a gentle walk. "And since I've no earthly notion where we are—by all means, have your head, ma'am."

CHAPTER **THREE**

The sun was at high noon when Keelock awoke in this place. They rode for hours across a plain like sun-cracked leather, broad and broken, the color of old bone, dotted with clusters of sage and rabbitbrush. Here and there a juniper hunched like a tired old man, roots stubbornly dug into rock-hard earth, but there was no sign of actual humanity. No signs, no trails, no wreckage or even rumors in the dust—only raw wilderness beneath the high vault of faded blue sky.

Now the light was dying and the world took on metallic hues as the sun bled behind distant mountains.

Overhead, black dots against the reddening sky resolved into buzzards circling as Keelock and the mare drew near the top of a crestline. The birds were the first sign of life Keelock had seen besides themselves. He slowed the horse, watching the birds. "Must be some good feed on," he said, tugging the reins to turn the mare's course. "Well, none of our busin—"

Pain hit him like a rifle round, sudden and devastating. He screamed, his hands flying to his throat and his body convulsing as he tumbled from the saddle. The mare sidestepped neatly, snorting, but undisturbed, as if this was all part of the natural order.

Keelock screamed and hit the ground hard, breath knocked clean from his lungs. His heels kicked as his body twisted, dust billowing around him while he writhed, choking and blinded. His fingers dug at his throat, scraping the already raw flesh as the ring of rope burn began to blaze like hellfire, lit from within and roaring through his veins, setting his every nerve alight. The mare watched with interest as the marks around Keelock's throat pulsed with light, glowing faintly, as if embers had been sealed inside of his skin.

He tried to crawl away, thrashing mindlessly as some instinct sought distance, but the agony was within him, stitched into his flesh. He flung himself sideways, fine grit grinding into his cheek, and screamed again, the sound rising and falling like a wounded animal, pouring from dust-choked lungs. Another lance of fire pierced him, arching his spine, nearly lifting him from the ground before he finally collapsed and darkness swallowed him again.

Keelock came to with a shuddering gasp, cool air raking his tortured lungs. The mare stood beside him, head dipped to nuzzle him with curiosity—or concern.

"Jesus," he whispered and rolled onto his back, staring upwards into a night-bruised, star-smeared sky. Every inch of his body throbbed and he was soaked in sweat, gone cold with the disappearance of the sun's warmth. Gingerly, he touched his throat. The burn marks were raw and pulsed warmly, but it was bearable now.

"Jesus Christ," he said again, half prayer and half curse. He pushed himself up with trembling arms, and climbed to his feet, staggering like a drunk before bracing himself against the horse, clutching the saddle. The mare stood patiently as he collected himself, breathing deeply for long moments.

Looking up at the sky, he asked aloud, "What the hell was that?"

The mare snorted and flicked her tail.

Keelock stooped to reclaim his hat, dusted it, then climbed into the saddle again, every movement stiff. Leaning forward, he ran a hand down the mare's neck, comforted by her warmth and her nearness. "I got the feeling you know something I don't, lady."

Her only answer was another soft snort.

"Figgers."

Keelock sat astride the mare, gathering his strength. He looked towards the sky, almost fully dark now, but still just light enough to see that that the buzzards were still circling something just beyond the ridge. If anything, there were more of them now and they were flying lower. Too low, and their circling had tightened. It was almost as if they weren't just waiting for something, but were watching.

He breathed deeply through his nose, and said, "Got a bad feelin' of where we're supposed to go," and touched the horse's flanks with his heels.

They climbed the ridge slowly, Keelock letting the mare find her own way. At the top, they paused and Keelock saw, on the other side, a dry arroyo, and in it sprawled the unmoving bodies of cattle, heaped atop one another by the dozen, maybe even the hundreds.

"God in heaven…" A shudder went down Keelock's spine.

Dismounting, his hand unconsciously fell to the empty holster on his hip. "My hat but not my damned gun, huh?"

He swore softly as he slid down the embankment and squatted beside one of the corpses. The cow's tongue lolled, its eyes open, but neither dry nor cloudy, and there wasn't a mark on it. No signs of violence or disease, but it was dead, without any doubt—the flesh was stiff and cold to the touch. Yet there wasn't the slightest bloating, which should have happened quickly beneath the heat of the plains, nor the faintest stink of rot.

"What the hell…?"

This many bodies, the air should have been thick enough with decay to wade through, and swarming with thousands of flies, but there were no insects and only the dry scent of the plains. This explained the buzzards, at least: they saw a feast laid out below them, but were chary enough to know something was very wrong and wise enough to keep their distance.

A faint rustling stirred the silence—a dry sound, like scales crawling over autumn leaves. It came from beneath the mound of bodies directly ahead of Keelock, as if something small and swift moved beneath the carcasses, slow and purposeful, stubbornly forcing its way through the dead weight. The mound of corpses shifted slightly, enough to let out the groan of hide rubbing hide, reminiscent of old harness leather.

Keelock pushed his hat back, leaned closer, pulse hammering, wishing for his gun—for any weapon.

Lightning tore the sky open, followed instantly by the sharp, angry crack of thunder directly overhead. For a split second, the shadows vanished—long enough for something small and fast to squirm from beneath the mounded cattle and scuttle quickly away, making a high, brittle chittering sound nearly lost in the thunder's fading echo.

Keelock whirled on his heel, trying to follow the movement, but saw nothing—only the shifting bodies of the dead and another flash overhead, casting the area in eerie light.

Keelock grit his teeth, his spine stiff, alert for anything, but without any hint of what might happen next.

"Hell with this," he muttered and turned towards the ridge.

As he climbed, the first drops of rain tapped his shoulders. The mare waited patiently, tail swishing, watching as he brushed dust from his denims.

Satisfied, he moved closer to the mare,

reaching for the reins. "Lady, if you know something, I really wish you'd just spit it out."

The horse whinnied.

"That's about what I thought you'd say."

He swung into the saddle. The rain came down steadily now. They made their way around the side of the arroyo, Keelock careful to keep his gaze dead ahead, well away from the mounded bodies. As they moved beyond the arroyo, leaving the dead behind, the storm grew, the rain falling in sheets, hissing as it pelted the dry ground.

The night was well along when Keelock finally spotted the trail—the first sign of man's presence in this weird country. It was well-used and easy to follow even in the storm. Before long, a sign appeared, leaning crookedly against the wind and rain. Lightning flashed, and Keelock read faded letters: BLACK ROCK →

He leaned forward in the saddle, peering through the downpour. He thought he saw distant lights flickering against the storm. "C'mon, girl," he said, urging the mare forward.

The trail became a heavily-trod road, hard enough that even the rain couldn't much dampen it, and soon shapes emerged from the night—buildings huddled together like tired cattle, waiting out the storm and the night. The nearest stood apart from the main body of the town, its lamplight beckoning from beneath a sign that read CAPSTONE SALOON.

Keelock guided the mare to the saloon's hitching post and swung down stiffly. He had found a rainslicker in the horse's saddlebags, but the storm proved its better. Rain found its way beneath the collar, down his back, soaking his jeans and seeping into his boots. The poor horse looked as miserable as he felt, huddled beneath the narrow overhang of the saloon's porch.

"Sorry, lady," he said, tying her off. "You earned better than this."

He stepped up onto the wooden porch, glad for its solidity beneath his feet and the roof over his head. He pushed through the batwing doors, water dripping from the brim of his hat and the oil-cloth coat. The interior of the place was warm, lit by oil-lamps and the glow of a potbellied stove off in one corner. The smell of damp and sawdust and stale beer filled the place and a low murmur of voices hummed all around.

"Whew!" Keelock breathed to the room at large. "One hell of a night out there, huh, fellas?"

He started to shed the slicker and stopped.

The place had gone silent. Every man in the saloon—the drinkers at the bar, the card players at the tables, the loners and drifters lurking in shadowed corners—each of them had a gun trained on him. Even the bartender leveled a double-barreled scattergun at him from behind the counter.

Keelock stood motionless, directly beneath the oil-lamp over the entrance, the brim of his hat casting his face in shadow. The heavy clicks of revolvers cocking and the dry snap of hammers pulled back chased each other around the room.

"Jesus Christ..." Keelock muttered. "The hell I walk into now?"

CHAPTER
FOUR

Keelock's hand went to his hip from long practice, but his fingertips touched only the worn leather of his empty holster, a reminder of his missing revolver that hit him like a slap. "Shiiit," he drawled, low and frustrated.

Slowly, he raised his hands to shoulder level, palms outward. "Now, hold on just a moment. Think I missed somethin' here." The heat of the room was already getting to him; he could feel sweat gathering beneath his collar as his eyes scanned those of the men in the room. Every set of eyes was on him, but no one would meet his gaze. There was something unwholesome about their silence, and the way they all stood still, weapons raised. It was as if they were united, but only by something brittle and foul that had drawn them together against their will.

"Maybe one of you fine gentlemen could—"

With a sound like a cleaver in a butcher's block, a sledgehammer fist crashed down on the nearest the table, making cards jump like startled birds and setting beer sloshing. Its owner, face red and glistening with sweat, growled, "God damn! The balls on this bastard!"

Keelock's gaze shifted. He saw a giant of a man, somewhere in his thirties, with a heavy tangled beard and arms thicker than the cottonwood branch Keelock had hanged from. The man's damp shirt clung to him, outlining a huge belly that Keelock knew would be hard as stone.

Another man—a kid, really, barely shaving and reminding Keelock of the boy from the posse—let his revolver fall out of line with Keelock, its muzzle drooping. Nerves and doubt were painted across his face. His eyes went to the man at the head of the room, who hadn't yet spoken. "You sure he's one of 'em, Mr. Garrity?" the boy asked. "He don't look like no Indian to me—or another one like that last drifter neither."

Keelock tried a thin smile, feigning calm, though his pulse hammered in his temples and there was a growing pressure behind his eyes, as if the turmoil inside of him was crowding his brainpan. "I assure you, son," he said evenly, "I ain't one like nobody."

Keelock barely registered the giant man's movement so swift was it. One moment he stood scowling and sweating, the next a freight train fist exploded across Keelock's jaw with the crack of meat on bone.

White-hot pain blurred Keelock's vision, its tendrils thrashing inside of his skull. His knees buckled, the floor lurched sideways, and he hit the boards hard, impact shivering up his spine as his teeth clacked together, clipping the tip of his tongue. The taste of blood filled his mouth, mixing with the grit of the plain that still clung to the back of his throat.

Colors swam before his eyes and he blinked several times, trying to clear them before he shifted to one side and spat blood and phlegm into the sawdust covering the floor. His breath shuddered out of him as he turned and saw the brute towering above him like a mountain of flesh, shovel hands clasped in front of him, cracking his knuckles one by one.

"You'll speak when spoken to," the giant said, calm and surprisingly quiet, though the menace was plain.

Keelock lay propped on an elbow, vision still loopy, looking up at the man. His head began to ring, and for an instant, the world dimmed, closing in around him as it had miles and hours ago, back on the ridge.

Something flared inside of him, not anger, or fear, but something colder and sharper—and older. Something that crouched inside of him waiting to erupt.

It began as a tremor beneath his skin, every inch of his body crawling, and became like a match struck against his spine, sending fire knifing upwards. He winced as heat surged through his back and neck, seeming to wrap around his throat like an unseen hand. His breath came hard, then not at all, and his skin tightened as his muscles convulsed. A tortured sound escaped his lips and his fingers clawed at his throat as the markings—the markings that were somehow both rope burn and the sign of that damned coyote—awoke with a searing light, pulsing beneath the skin like molten wire.

The kid with the revolver stepped back, a shudder running through him. "Holy shit…"

Keelock's body jerked and spasmed, his breathing sharp and ragged, his throat constricting until the air wheezed in and out like struggling bellows. Light flared inside of his skull, eliminating all shreds of darkness just before his vision narrowed to a tunnel of flickering orange and crimson.

The room peeled away. Everything in the saloon—the suspicious gunmen, their rage, their fear, the smells of beer and sweat and coal oil and wet clothing, and Keelock's own blood in the sawdust—it all unraveled like scorched parchment. Space folded in on itself as time tilted, running sideways and backwards and crossways as Keelock plunged into the dark hollows of memory.

Another saloon squatted in the dust, its adobe walls hard-baked but cracked with age. If it had a name, it was long forgotten, but the air inside was cool after the heat of the trail.

The place was nearly empty. A man dressed in buck hide snored softly in the corner furthest from the entrance, slumped against his table, face down in spilled beer. Another stood at the bar, nursing his own beer, using only his left hand, keeping his right free at all times.

The batwing doors creaked as Keelock stepped into the cool dimness, heels of his boots echoing faintly. He spoke softly, but it was loud in the stillness. "Jay Cooley."

The drinker at the bar turned just enough to show Keelock a smirk. "Well, if it ain't Keelock the horse-thief."

Keelock's jaw tensed, but he didn't immediately respond. He moved to the end of the bar, deliberately keeping distance between himself and Cooley. The silent, empty room felt like it was watching them both.

"Yep," Keelock muttered finally. "That's the same shit you been spewing all over, I reckon."

He set his elbow on the bar and looked down its length at the other man. "You got a problem with me, Cooley, why not come say it to my face 'stead of makin' me chase your trail?"

Cooley took another slow drink, then licked foam from his lip. "Me find you?" He made a scoffing noise. "Only reason I'd look for a horse-thief is to string him up."

Keelock shook his head. "I don't know where you got this idea, Cooley, and I sure as hell don't appreciate your talk. I bought that horse months ago, two-hundred-some-odd miles from here."

"Funny thing," Cooley said, staring at his own reflection in the warped mirror back of the bar, "how much that cayuse you say you've had for so long looks just like the one went missing from the Why-Squared range a couple weeks ago." He turned, showing Keelock that hateful little smile.

"Ain't it?"

A long, tired sigh left Keelock. He shifted slightly and gestured toward the bartender, a tall thin man in an apron, as he entered from a side door, hefting a crate of bottles. Setting the crate on the bar with a rattle of glass, he eyed the two men but said nothing.

"Cooley," Keelock said, voice low now. "If a body didn't know any better, he'd swear you were just lookin' for trouble." To the bartender, never taking his eyes from Cooley, he added, "Been a spell, Ed. Gimme a shot of that top-shelf rye, huh?"

"Sure, Ben." The bartender nodded and turned his back, reaching toward one of the highest shelves.

"Let's settle this once and for all, Cooley."

Cooley drained the last of his beer and set the mug down hard.

"I hate to waste good horse flesh," Keelock continued, "but since you're so stuck on it—you pay me what that gelding's worth, and we'll take a look at the underside of his hide, see if the brand's been altered. That's the only way I know to settle this amiable-like."

Cooley let out a dry chuckle. "Oh, I can think of a way I'd be amiable to. And besides—"

His arm jerked, and a pistol barrel slid from beneath his elbow, just below the level of the bar, angled up and steadied on Keelock. "I'd rather see the inside of your hide."

The gun roared, but Keelock was already moving. His own revolver appeared in his hand like magic and he fanned the hammer rapidly, trading three shots for Cooley's one.

The first shot went wide, cracking glass, but the second tore into Cooley's shoulder, spinning him half-around just before the last punched in under his ribs. Cooley dropped his gun and collapsed.

Behind the bar, Ed turned, bottle in hand, eyes wide. "Jesus—"

Keelock said nothing. Smoke curled from the barrel of his gun and his heart pounded in his chest. Reaction was already setting in. Gunplay was familiar, but never welcome.

Ed leaned forward to peer over the top of the bar. Cooley's body had fallen forward, face-down.

The bartender exhaled, the sound neither sigh nor groan, but carrying the meaning of both. "I know you ain't no back-shooter, Ben, but the way this looks," he said, "you best ride."

Ben Keelock rode. They caught him in a wash, surrounding him and hauling him down from his horse in a tangle of limbs and curses, and hanged him from that lonely tree—and then the dark swallowed him whole, wrapping him in suffocating velvet for must have been an eon.

The world shifted again, shredding, the pieces skirling in a wind like a moan from the cracked and bleeding lips of some forgotten god. Keelock opened his eyes and found himself standing in a narrow valley ringed by dead hills, the sky above ashen, filled with racing clouds that moved at the speed of thought. It wasn't night, nor was it day—the place was a colorless, timeless purgatory.

Keelock stepped a few paces to his left,

then his right, his boots crunching against brittle bones and splinters of charred wood. The ground was scorched black, ruined. Nothing grew here and nothing moved except the wind, tugging at his clothing like an urchin begging for coin.

His limbs tingled and his stomach felt hollow. He didn't know this place's name, couldn't find it on any map, but he knew it—if not how he knew.

The memory took shape slowly, welling up from the recesses of his mind as blood slowly seeps from an infected wound. He looked around, trying to identify familiar shapes, and spotted, several yards away, the beams of the old structure jutting from the earth like broken ribs. He moved to inspect it, squatting on his heels, sifting ashes with his hands. The ash was not only cold, it was so old that it had settled into a fine powder.

Keelock stood, images of the place as it once was flooding his mind, as if transferred through the ashes by some strange osmosis: people in their best clothing, a man in a black suit and backwards collar, leading grouped families in song. This was a church—or what was left of one. He spun in a slow circle, looking all around him, spotting the details in the remains now that he knew what he was seeing. Fire had gutted the place long ago and what hadn't burned had collapsed into a heap of twisted pews and ash-choked boards. All four walls had collapsed, the roof crumpled inwards, the steeple snapped off to half-bury itself in the dead earth like a fallen spear.

Keelock's stomach turned. This wasn't just memory of disaster. This was the echo of judgment—or bitter hatred.

He stepped forward, his boots stirring the ash, rising up and swirling into phantom shapes—faces he couldn't quite recognize and voices lost in the wind. He heard a woman's sob and a child's laugh that turned to screaming. He could smell burning hair and burning skin.

Shivers went through him, warring with the strangle tingling in his limbs, leaving an empty space somewhere inside of him that made him wonder why it was there to begin with. It wasn't his—it couldn't be.

Slowly, Keelock became aware of the whispers, soft at first, creeping into his brain like worms through rot.

"You gave no warning, gave them no chance..."

"She begged you..."

"They all did."

"You earned this."

Keelock's breath grew shallow and convulsive. The wind kicked up, seeming to carry the whispers away, but bringing something new—a sharp, coppery scent. Blood, freshly spilled.

He whirled on his heel, feeling for the first time as if he wasn't alone, and saw a door. It stood upright in the center of the ruins—freestanding, connected to nothing but itself. Its frame was blackened, warped with heat, and yet the brass handle gleamed like it had been polished just that morning.

He moved closer, drawn despite himself, and slowly became aware of the sounds from behind it: footsteps, slow and heavy.

Keelock backed away, hand searching his hip for his lost weapon.

The door creaked open, an inch at a time. Smoke curled out, thick and clinging. Obscured by the smoke, something stepped through—a silhouette framed in flickering red light. It was tall, hooded, cloaked in darkness deeper than the world around it. Beneath the hood, eyes like emeralds glowed with some inner light, finding and fixing on Keelock.

It spoke in a voice like an empty tomb. "You thought you could ride from this? Leave it all behind, as if it never was?"

Keelock stumbled, bile rising in his throat, burning him from the inside as the rope marks burned without. The earth trembled and then split beneath his feet with the sound of breaking bones and then he was falling again.

The world stretched and snapped like wet hide recoiling. Colors smeared and shapes distorted, sending fingers of fire plunging into his skull until suddenly—

He hit the saloon floor like a corpse dropped from a hangman's scaffold, gasping, soaked with sweat.

CHAPTER FIVE

The vision was gone. Keelock was back in the real world—or what passed for it. He was still unsure. It could all be one final spark inside his dying mind as he hung from that old cottonwood. But the mountainous man still loomed over him, the brooding menace gone now, replaced by confusion. The pain of that huge fist had felt real enough at least.

Keelock thought back, reliving the vision in his mind's eye in an instant. Cooley he remembered, of course. The shooting, the chase, the hanging—he remembered all of it. But the burned church? "What the hell…?" Those weren't his memories.

His gaze rose to see the kid staring hard, revolver held in both hands now, but still shaking in his grip. His fear was as plain as a fresh brand. The boy half-turned as the man he had called Garrity stepped forward slowly, eyes narrowing.

"What in God's name was that?" Garrity asked, both suspicion and awe in his voice. There was fear too, but he carried it better than the kid.

Keelock opened his mouth to answer, but no words came. His throat was still tight and his tongue felt swollen, as it had when he was hanged. He shook his head slowly, a hand going to his neck. The wounds from the rope were still there, still raw and painful, but there was something else, too—something beneath them, something hot and wild that even then was retreating, folding itself into some hidden place.

He rose to his feet, a man dragging himself from his own grave. His body screamed, his muscles aching. Sweat and blood stung his eyes. A murmur passed through the saloon, but died just as quickly, as if everyone held their breath, waiting to see what this stranger would do next. Keelock wiped the back of his hand across his face, pushing sweat and dirt and blood aside, then stooped with deliberate slowness to retrieve his fallen hat.

The brute who had struck him took a single step backwards. For the first time, the scowl was gone, replaced by uncertainty. "What the hell are you?" he asked thickly.

"Mad," Keelock answered, the toe of his boot flashing out, impacting the man's crotch with a sickening thud. The huge man folded with a howl, doubling over before collapsing to the floor, gasping for breath and twitching in the sawdust.

Keelock stood straight and still, hat in

hand. His eyes found the boy, pistol held in a white-knuckled grip, and then shifted to the old man called Garrity. The blood was gone from the man's face and for a moment, his mouth worked as if all intelligence had left him. He looked as if he had recognized a face from some ancient nightmare.

His lips trembled as he spoke. "That mark… That thing on your neck—the devil's handiwork!"

Keelock said nothing, but the mark answered for him. He could feel it beneath his skin, beneath the rope burns, no longer blazing, but still hot and wild—only temporarily calmed. The memory of the coyote, seeming to grin at him, flashed through his mind. "The damned dog put me on a leash," he whispered.

"What are you?" Garrity asked.

"Something's wrong, Mr. Garrity," the boy said, finally slipping his gun into its holster. "This fella seems honest to God as confused as the rest of us and even…" He looked at Keelock almost shyly. "Even with what happened, he really don't seem like one of 'em." Keelock wondered what they had seen during his vision.

A voice rang out from above—sharp, female, and angry. "Of course he isn't one of them, you damned fools!"

Keelock turned. On the second-floor balcony stood a finely dressed woman, leaning over the railing. She was somewhere in her thirties, Keelock guessed, and handsome, though at that moment, her face was all frustration and fire.

"Does that fellow look like any Indian you ever saw?" she snapped to the room as a whole.

The crowd shifted uncomfortably, looking from the woman to Keelock, then throwing glances at one another.

One man, chicken-necked and pock-faced, called back to her from the foot of the stairs. "Miss Mason, if he ain't with them Injuns, what the hell's he doin' in this shithole town right when there's trouble?"

The woman descended the stairs with purpose, skirts gathered in one hand, the other on the railing. There was no haste in her movements. Keelock felt she almost glided so graceful was the way she walked. And she was clearly used to commanding attention. Every eye in the room, including Keelock's, followed her, drawn like iron filings to a magnet.

"Same as the rest of you buffoons at the moment, I imagine," Miss Mason said coolly as she reached the bottom step. "Trying to stay out of the rain."

The gathered men murmured but moved aside as she passed. She stopped near the bar and turned to face Keelock. The crowd instinctively parted, leaving a clear line of sight between them. Her eyes fixed on him.

"What's your name, mister?"

Keelock's eyes narrowed. For the briefest moment, Mason's face wasn't her own. Overlayed in his mind was another woman's image: a younger woman, but with the same eyes, dressed in a dancehall girl's feathered finery.

Can't be…

"Keelock," he said, his throat suddenly dry.

"You an Indian-lover, Mr. Keelock?" The woman's tone didn't change.

The saloon went still. Keelock didn't look around, but he felt the weight of the men's stares on him—every bastard in that room was waiting for his answer and it would decide what they did next.

He glanced sideways, then back to Mason. "I ain't exactly a lover of anyone at the moment, ma'am."

Miss Mason smiled. "That's probably as good an answer as any."

She turned toward the bar, saying over the noise of the muttering crowd, "Arthur! A bottle of brandy, please."

She started up the stairs again. Halfway, she turned and gestured toward Keelock. "Mr. Keelock, if you'll come with me, I'll see if we can find you a towel and a glass."

Garrity, finally recovered from his shock, stabbed a finger toward the stairs. "Hold on there, Bethany! What d'you think you're—"

Miss Mason's voice remained level as she said, "Anything I damned well please in my own god-damned saloon, Garrity."

The men quieted like whipped dogs. Mason looked down towards Keelock, who eyed the double-barrel laying across the bar as he accepted a bulbous-necked bottle from the barkeeper. She nodded her thanks to Arthur and said, "Now come along, Mr. Keelock."

Keelock's eyes swept the room. The men were still clearly hostile, suspicious—and rightfully so, he decided. One of the men mentioned trouble and Indians. How anyone could mistake Keelock for an Indian was beyond him, but these men were scared, and scared men only needed an excuse to lash out. Still, they clearly respected Mason and none of them made any move as he followed her.

"Sure thing," he muttered, cradling the brandy and climbing the stairs.

The upstairs hall smelled of old wood, smoke, and faint lavender. Mason led Keelock into a parlor stuffed with heavy, overstuffed furniture, closing the door behind them. The room glowed with firelight from a cast-iron stove and a single oil-lamp. A velvet curtain rustled as the wind and rain pawed at the windows. A faint draft came from the window, but the stove more than overcame it.

The woman's manner shifted, softening slightly as she spoke. "I apologize for my customers, Mr. Keelock. Those damned fools won't admit it, but they're scared stiff."

"I know. I can practically smell it on 'em." Keelock scratched at a trickle of dried blood on his temple, still tasting copper in his mouth. "But what're they so scared of, Miss… uh—"

"Mason," she said, gesturing to a pair of wingback chairs. "Bethany Mason. Please, let me take your slicker. You need to dry off and warm up." She produced a pair of brandy glasses from a low cabinet and set them on the table between the two chairs.

Keelock slipped from the slicker, handing it to Miss Mason. The woman hung it by the stove as he poured two fingers of brandy into each glass. The liquor caught the room's dim light, glowing like liquid gold.

Sinking into one of the chairs, he said, "I'm much obliged for your hospitality, Miss Mason, and I hope you'll forgive me for being so blunt—"

Mason cut him off with a knowing smile. "'But what the hell is going on around here?' That about right?" In a rustle of skirts, she slipped into the chair opposite him and lifted one of the glasses.

Keelock grunted, taking a sip of the liquor. It burned his throat, but not like the rope or the markings. This was familiar, reminding him that he was alive, even if he felt half-dead.

Mason studied him over her glass, hers eyes clearly appraising. "May I ask about your neck, Mr. Keelock?"

His hand drifted there instinctively. "Uh…"

"Well, never mind. Go ahead and keep your secrets," she said, settling her glass in her lap. She seemed amused now. "I think I already know everything about you that I need to."

He looked up at her, wary. "How's that, ma'am?"

She stood without hurry, placing her glass on the side table. "Why this, of course—"

She lifted his slicker from where it hung, turning it inside-out. The firelight revealed the stylized, grinning coyote head, stitched on the inside of the garment like a hidden brand.

Mason's voice was almost cheery as she asked, "Am I mistaken about how you came by this, Mr. Keelock?"

He stared at it grimly, somehow unsurprised. "Reckon not. Only how—?"

"They never tell us," she said, folding the

slicker closed again and replacing it on the hook above the stove. Her smile was unreadable. "It would ruin their fun, I imagine."

Keelock opened his mouth, but a thunderous crash split the air, rattling the windows and shaking dust from the ceiling beams. Mason flinched as the sound came again, changing into a deep-throated rumble that shook the building. Keelock sprang for the door, brandy and cold and damp clothing forgotten as he stepped onto the balcony.

The building shook like dice in a cup and below, the saloon had erupted into chaos. Chairs and tables were toppled as men shouted, fought, and scrambled over one another, trying to find escape or a place of concealment. Pure bedlam had overtaken them in their panic. Only Arthur remained calm, standing alone behind the bar like a captain refusing to leave his sinking ship.

"What the hell is that shaking?" Keelock shouted over the steadily mounting noise.

Arthur's voice rose above the madness, his eyes on the balcony. "Stampede!"

Mason had appeared at Keelock's side. They exchanged a look. Something passed between them—and then they ran.

They raced down the stairs, past the jumble of flailing limbs and spilled drinks. Keelock shoved a stumbling man aside, clearing a path for Miss Mason. The front doors bucked on their hinges, wind and earth pounding behind them like the approach of a vengeful army.

Outside, the storm still lashed the sky, driving rain battering the packed-dirt street as near-continuous lightning turned the scene into a flickering nightmare. Horses tied to the rail screamed in hysterical fear, fighting their reins, wanting nothing but escape.

And through the storm came the cattle. Hundreds of them, flooding the road like a dark, living river. They lowed, their eyes rolled, their hooves thundered, and among them—

Shapes.

Small, black things clung to the backs of a number of the beasts. Wrong-sized, hunched, their presence more felt than seen, but Keelock knew they were there. More than that, they were familiar in the worst way—the things of childhood terrors.

Keelock turned to Mason, her face pale in the lightning's flash. "I think you better tell me exactly what's happening in this town."

CHAPTER
SIX

Keelock rode hard through the night, the rain lashing his face like tiny whips. The storm and the stampede had turned the trail into muck, causing the horse to fight for every step, but he pushed her forward, ignoring the sting of wind and water against his face. His slicker clung to him, already soaked through again, the weight of it pulling at his shoulders, making his skin both clammy and itchy. The wind howled as if it was hunting something—probably him.

"Got to get—" he muttered breathlessly, as if he were the one running through the darkness.

He opened his slicker enough to see, suspended on a rawhide cord around his neck, that the pendant still hung there. It was small, no bigger than a silver dollar, with the familiar woven shape of an Indian charm—a dreamcatcher—but it felt older somehow and wilder, as if there was something inside straining for release. He felt a strange kinship with the pendant, as if part of it belonged to him before he ever laid eyes on it. He fingered it gently and at his touch, the woven strands glowed with a weak light.

"Got to get closer," Keelock finished. The pendant glowed a little brighter.

His mind went back to the porch of the saloon, back in Black Rock, as he tried to order his thoughts.

Miss Mason stood beside him, silent and almost deathly still, looking towards the edge of town where the plains fell into darkness and the stampeding cattle had disappeared. Her lips were parted and her head slightly tilted in an attitude of listening, as if she could hear a voice Keelock couldn't. As he watched her, something seemed to shimmer behind her eyes, gone too quickly for him to be sure. She had turned to another point in the darkness then, and fixed on it as if she were matching her gaze with something that crouched just beyond the light, waiting for its chance.

Keelock snapped from his moment of reverie, wiping a hand across his mouth before asking, "What exactly is happening in this town, Miss Mason?"

Mason didn't look at him, but he knew from the way her posture shifted that whatever she had experienced was gone now too. "You should already know, Mr. Keelock."

She met his gaze at last. "If he sent you here—"

"I don't know a God-damned thing!" Keelock snapped, his voice rising along with his temper. He was sick of mysteries, tired of feeling lost. He ached to be riding herd again, patching fence, to be doing anything he knew and was accustomed to.

"You think I'm any part of this?" he asked. "I just want to get out with my head still attached." Unconsciously, his hand went to his damaged throat.

A calm as a prairie dusk, Mason turned and walked back into the saloon. "Come with me," she said over her shoulder.

The mostly empty saloon was a shambles after the stampede's shaking and the mass of fearful men that had rampaged through it. Arthur stood implacable behind the bar, polishing a glass, and a couple of the men who remained moved around the room, righting chairs and tables.

Mason ignored it all, the wreckage of her saloon, the men left behind, and climbed the stairs. Keelock followed.

Inside Miss Mason's private rooms, she lit a second oil lamp, hung it from a hook in one corner and moved to a cabinet. The cabinet door opened with a faint creak as she said, "Coyote sent you."

Just hearing the name aloud sent tingles of frustration and trickles of fear through Keelock. He shook his head. "That was a dream," he said, trying to convince himself and failing.

"That was—" he started again, but remembered the agony of the noose around his neck and what the coyote had said: "You need a miracle, and I need a favor…"

Mason turned, a revolver in hand—a long-barreled Colt .45, silvered and etched with markings that caught the lamplight and seemed to trap it, shifting like mercury, inside of itself. Keelock recognized some of the etchings, drawn from whites' religions and superstitions: a dove, the all-seeing eye of God, a simple cross. Others he didn't recognize, but could guess at their origin. Lots of Indian tribes had stories about old Coyote, didn't they?

"Are those marks on your neck a dream, Mr. Keelock?" Mason asked. "The brand on that horse you ride? Or the figure stitched into the lining of your slicker?"

Keelock faltered. "I... don't know," he muttered. "God damn it... why is this—"

"Here." She pressed the revolver into his hands.

He stared down at it—the weapon was heavy, not just its weight, but in the meaning it carried.

"You'll need this," she said.

Keelock didn't want it—he wanted no more of this strangeness. He knew that wasn't an option. He had gotten his miracle, and fair was fair, wasn't it?

He holstered the gun with a grunt, grateful at least for the familiar weight on his hip.

"Thanks, I suppose," he said. "Felt a little naked without one."

Mason stepped closer, her hand going to a rawhide thong around her neck that Keelock hadn't noticed before. From beneath the bodice of her dress, she drew the pendant. "And you'll need this too."

She lifted the hat from his head. He stiffened, caught off guard by the sudden act, by its familiarity. She settled the pendant over his neck, her fingers brushing his skin, warm despite the chill of standing outside so long in the storm.

"Miss Mason…"

"I don't have answers for you, Mr. Keelock," she said. "Except that you're here because, for some reason all its own, Coyote chose you. And because there are children who need you."

"Children?" he asked, confused.

Mason nodded and her eyes seemed to darken. "Every little girl and boy from town and the farms and the ranches around the country... gone."

She turned from him, voice tight. "A lot of folks want to blame the Indians—though I reckon Indian kids are missing too, if anybody cared to ask."

"I don't understand. The cattle and those... those things—"

"It doesn't matter if you understand or not," she said. "What matters is that you find those kids. I know that's why Coyote sent you—there can't be any other reason for your being here."

Keelock looked up at the ceiling as if he could find answers there—or maybe divine guidance. Somewhere, miles above, stars were burning and the moon would be shining, easing the weight of the night. But down here, there was only darkness and it seemed to grow heavier with each passing minute.

"Even if I accept all that—and I ain't sayin' I do—how would I even start to—"

The pendant against his chest flared to life, glowing through the wet cloth of his shirt.

"Mr. Keelock," she said quietly, "I think you just need to follow."

CHAPTER SEVEN

The rain had grown meaner, almost vicious now, as if the harder Keelock rode, the harder it fought him. It slashed sideways, stinging Keelock's face like thousands of ice-cold razors. His slicker hung heavy with water, dragging at his limbs, but he rode on, the ghost-glow of the pendant flickering through the folds of oilskin, the only light in the world as far as Keelock could tell. He had no idea what he was riding towards, but at least he wouldn't lose his way: the pendant glowed more brightly when he traveled in the direction it wanted him to go and the marks on his neck burned like hellfire if he purposely tried to turn away. He wouldn't repeat that experiment.

Thunder cracked directly overhead, a deep-throated, bone-rattling rumble, that seemed to tear the very sky apart. For a heartbeat the country was thrown into stark silhouette by lightning flash. Keelock saw ahead, rising from the earth like the back of some ancient, buried leviathan, a massive black mountain. Its peak vanished into a writhing ceiling of storm-cloud, lost to shadow and God's own fury.

Abruptly, the trail turned steep. Crossing the plain, the trail had been muck and mud, torn by the passage of hundreds of charging hooves, but it remained recognizable even in the dark. Now it was like nature was trying to reclaim what man had worn, leaving the trail slick with moss and shale, dotted with twisted trees that clung to the slope like black phantoms who didn't realize they were dead. Keelock reined in hard, his boots dragging, the horse whinnying and restless beneath him.

A rifle shot split the air.

The sound snapped something inside of Keelock. He kicked free of the stirrups and hit the rocky ground hard, rolling as another shot hissed past his skull.

"Christ!" The storm drowned his voice.

He crawled behind the horse for what cover her body could provide. The poor animal shrieked, eyes wild as she stamped her hooves. Keelock knew how she felt.

Keelock spied past the horse's flank, both man and horse soaked to the bone, breathing hard, and shaking with both cold and adrenaline. He squinted into the darkness uselessly. Whoever was out there was well hidden by the night and the storm.

Cupping hands to mouth, Keelock

shouted, "Who in hell is that? Show your face, you God-damned bushwhackin' son of a bitch!"

Lightning flashed again, the thunder directly overhead, and in its instant of brilliance, Keelock saw him: the same big bastard who had laid him flat back in the saloon. There was no mistaking that bulk as the gigantic man crouched high on the ridge, rifle braced against one knee.

"Keelock!" the man howled like a banshee, drawing the name out before the rifle roared again, fire belching from its muzzle.

With a cry of terror, the horse's nerve finally broke and she went pattering back down the slope, leaving Keelock in the open. He scrambled, almost slipping in a patch of mud as he dove behind a slab of broken rock, barely the size of a coffin lid. Dirt exploded where he had just been. Even through the storm, the stink of burnt powder filled Keelock's nostrils. The man on the ridge was a hell of a shot.

"Friend," Keelock barked, "I don't know your name or what kind of game you think you're playin'—"

Another shot snapped past Keelock, making him wince and duck back behind the rock. He pulled his slicker aside and yanked free the revolver Mason had given him. Something seemed to pass from the weapon into Keelock and he relished the feel of it in his hand: solid and cold and heavy as sin.

"And I really ain't lookin' to do any shootin' on a night like this—" he called, stepping out into the open, eyes narrowed against the storm. The pendant's glow pulsed beneath his clothing like a heartbeat as he raised the pistol, trusting to instinct and whatever luck the weapon possessed.

"But I'm comin' through, one way or another!" he roared and began fanning the hammer, shots racing upwards as muzzle flashes tore the darkness.

Answering gunfire cracked in return, the rifle rounds slicing the air, but biting only mud and bark and pitting stone all around Keelock. He broke into a sprint up the incline, weaving through wet brush and jagged rock, boots skidding, mud sucking at his heels, nearly losing his balance with every other step. "I mean it, fella! You ain't stoppin' me!"

He hunched behind a gnarled pine, chest heaving from the uphill dash, and snapped open the cylinder to feed the weapon fresh cartridges. He looked up towards where the rifleman had crouched, rain sliding down his face in rivulets. He realized that, aside from the storm, the mountain had grown quiet.

Keelock rose to his feet, snapping the revolver's cylinder into place and drawing the hammer back with his thumb. His every nerve was taut as piano wire, and wary of trickery, he was ready to spring in any direction. "You still there, friend? Ain't tryin' to Indian down on me, are you?"

Lightning ripped the sky and in that bright white moment, Keelock saw him. The big man was still crouched up the slope, but the rifle was slack in his hands, his mouth hung open—and he wasn't alone.

Small, black things moved behind the rifleman. Not men or animals. They could be children maybe, but they would have to be the spawn of the devil himself. By lightning flash, Keelock saw twisted, hunched things with arms too long and legs bent all wrong, their heads misshapen. He only caught a glimpse of one of the things' faces in the instant of lightning, but it looked like melted wax. Nightmare things, yet he recognized them: the creatures who had ridden the stampeding cattle.

In that fractional moment before the darkness slammed down again, Keelock took the scene in and made a decision.

He charged uphill, his boots slipping, his heart hammering against his sternum, crossing half a dozen yards before the rifle roared. The scream that followed didn't sound human and echoed all around him, bouncing off bare stone and stunted trees that seemed to magnify the sound until it was loud enough to batter his nerves. "Holy hell!" he blurted, resisting the urge to cover his ears.

Keelock reached the spot where he judged the rifleman had been—and found nothing. He spun, revolver raised, narrowed eyes trying to pierce the night and storm. "Now where'd he get to?"

His foot struck something firm, but yielding. He knelt, holstered his gun as he fished in his pocket, then struck a match against his boot. Sheltered by his other hand, the flame trembled in the rain and wind, casting a pathetically small glow.

It was enough. The giant rifleman lay flat on his back, staring into the sky, eyes wide and wet and empty. His face was twisted in agony, his lips pulled back from his teeth, and his jaw clenched. But Keelock saw no wound, not a drop of blood or a mark on him.

"Christ Almighty…" Keelock whispered. "Just like them cattle."

Something moved behind him as the match fizzled out.

Without realizing he was doing it, Keelock reached instinctively for the pendant, fingers clutching it through his soaked clothing. It flared, bright and sudden, lighting the slope like a lantern inside a barrel.

Keelock stood in a madman's hell. There were dozens of them, surrounding him on all sides. Child-sized horrors, all wrong and all watching him with black, glittering eyes. Their skin was slick and mottled black, like bone dipped in crude oil, and their faces were human, but warped, pained, the features seeming almost liquid. One and all, they grinned, showing far too many teeth as they crouched in a ring around him, unmoving, simply waiting.

"Christ Almighty…" he said again, more prayer than curse this time.

A shot cracked and one of the creatures' heads snapped back, splitting like a rotten pumpkin, spewing the slope with gore.

Keelock wheeled toward the sound. The light of the pendant barely reached where Garrity, the old man from the saloon, stood, half-shadowed beneath a copse of scraggly trees. He looked like he had crawled from the bottom of some swamp. His clothes were torn and stained with mud that even the driving rain hadn't washed away. A Winchester repeater was snugged against his shoulder, aimed downslope. His eyes were wide, unblinking.

Something feral burned inside of them.

"Garrity!"

"That shot," the old man growled back, voice ragged beneath the sound of the storm, "was meant for you, Keelock!"

The creatures' heads snapped towards Garrity with insectile precision, black eyes gleaming like wet oilstone. A rising chorus of clicks and chittering spread across the night, competing with the ruckus of the storm, the sound like the rustle of grave beetles beneath a corpse's skin. Nausea swirled through Keelock.

There was an instant's pause, as if a decision were being made—and then they moved.

The swarm surged up the slope in a wave of black limbs and gnashing teeth. Garrity's eyes went wide and a cry of surprise and terror escaped him. He raised the Winchester and fired blindly, the muzzle flare giving Keelock staccato glimpses of his pale, rain-slicked face as he pumped the lever and pulled the trigger over and over.

"Back, God damn you!" Garrity shouted, but his voice cracked, edging higher with each word.

He moved awkwardly up the slope, trying to maintain footing without sight of where he was going. He made it several futile steps before one foot slipped on wet shale, skinny rump slamming hard into the stone and his body following. The rifle skidded from his grasp, disappearing in the dark—and then the creatures were on him.

Keelock heard the wet thump of tiny fists impacting flesh and then the tearing of teeth and claws. Garrity's scream blared like a freight whistle:

"Keelock! Keelock! For the love of God—call off your monsters!"

Keelock froze, the rain hammering his hat brim, as the idea hammered his already battered thoughts. "My monsters?"

Even the idea made his guts curdle, but he shook it off, bellowing, "Garrity! Hold on!"

Revolver raised, he surged up the incline, boots repeatedly slipping, but managing to keep his footing. As he drew closer, the pendant flared beneath his rain-drowned clothing like a living thing, casting its ghost-light in all directions. The swarm shrieked in protest at the glow, scattering like cockroaches at sight of a torch. Their chittering faded into the thin brush, moving higher up the mountain, leaving behind only silence, rain—and the wreckage they had wrought.

Keelock dropped to a knee beside Garrity. The older man lay half-curled, clothes shredded, his face torn raw, streaked with gore. One eye was crushed in its socket, leaking blood and a milky fluid. The other stared at Keelock, fever-bright and haunted. However they killed the cattle and the big man, it hadn't been with violence. The old man had aroused their fury.

Cuz he killed one of 'em, Keelock thought.

Keelock reached out a hand. "Here, man, let me help you—"

Garrity's own hand, trembling and bloodied, lashed out, swatting Keelock away. "Keep your filthy God-damned paws off me!"

Keelock recoiled, a mixture of emotions swirling inside of him as he watched the old man force himself up with a ragged grunt. He felt anger, pity, disgust.

Rubbing viciously at his ruined eye with the back of one hand, Garrity swept the area, finally spotting his rifle just at the edge of the pendant's light. He limped towards the fallen weapon, but Keelock beat him to it.

The two men stared at one another a moment. Rain sluiced down Garrity's face, mixing with his blood. If he ever had a hat, it was long gone.

Keelock tried to avoid looking at the ruined eye, but some sick fascination drew his gaze to it. Garrity, in his shock, hadn't seemed to notice yet. It would hurt like hell when he came around, Keelock mused, his pity of the old man growing.

But pity got them nowhere. The pendant's light was fading again and Keelock had the feeling time was growing short.

Keelock shoved the rifle out, butt-first. "What's your problem with me, Garrity?"

"Like you don't know, you devilish bastard," Garrity spat, eyeing his weapon a moment before taking it back, almost reluctantly, as if Keelock's touch had fouled it.

"I ain't got a clue!" Keelock snapped, his voice harsh. "I haven't understood one God damn thing since that noose tightened around my throat. I wish to Christ that damned Coyote had just let me hang."

The name hit the air like a thunderclap.

Garrity had turned away, but now he froze. "Coyote?"

He shifted back to look at Keelock, sidestepping to put distance between them. The man's hands shook as the rifle slowly rose. Hatred glinted in his good eye. "So you're with that one, are you? Now it's startin' to make some sense, by God."

Keelock raised his hands to shoulder-level, left palm out, the revolver pointed towards the sky. "Put that damned thing down, Garrity. You saved me, whether you meant to or not, and I reckon I just returned the favor. Don't that earn me a mite of trust?"

For a long moment, neither spoke, and nothing moved except the rain pattering on stone and earth and gun-metal.

Garrity's shoulders slumped as he let the rifle dip. "Hell," he muttered. "Suppose you could've let 'em chew me up."

Keelock gave a weary nod and lowered his hands. He holstered the revolver and asked, "What's this about another fella?"

Garrity's jaw worked. "You really don't know?"

"Already told you—I don't know shit."

Garrity hocked and spat blood into the darkness. He wiped the back of his hand against his mouth, examining what he found. "You don't know nothing about them critters? Nothing about that fella raving about some God-damned war between your Coyote and—"

A sound from above cut him off—a deep rolling peal that echoed like thunder, but with a tone that hit the eardrums all wrong.

As if on cue, both men looked towards the sky as lightning seared the darkness. For one breathless instant, they saw it. High above them, black against the flash, colossal wings were spread wide enough to blot out the clouds. The silhouette was too enormous to be real, and too real to be anything but a massive bird. A dark, immense bird born of this nightmare they were trapped in.

"Crow," Garrity said in an awed whisper.

CHAPTER
EIGHT

Keelock grabbed Garrity by the collar, barking, "Down!" and threw them both into the mud just as the sky split with a hellish screech.

They hit hard, the bird's scream whirling about them like a whip of sound as the huge, black form passed overhead. Keelock flattened his body against the earth, the scents of blood and mud and thunder thick in his nostrils. Beside him, Garrity's head twisted upwards, defying reason and sanity, his one eye locked on the shape slicing through the murk and the storm.

"That's him, Keelock!" he shouted over the roar. "That's the one!"

Keelock twisted to follow the old man's line of sight. The massive bird—black and unnatural in a way that went beyond just its size—climbed toward the peak of the mountain, wings carving the air like scythes.

"That's who?" he asked.

"Didn't you see 'im? Right atop that God-damned bird, ridin' like you or I'd ride a horse! He was the one rantin' 't'other day," Garrity breathed, "about coyotes and crows—"

*

The climb would be rough in good weather. Storm and mud and the broken shale littering the slope made it near impossible. But Keelock fought upwards, alone, each step a battle he had to win. His boots were made for riding, not walking and his feet ached. He was exhausted and unprepared for this—for any of it. The hand of the mountain, and its cold breath on his neck, reminded him of those facts every chance it got.

He barely noticed any of it. "Coyotes and crows." The words echoed in his head, like some insistent imp perched on his shoulder, whispering in his ear, determined that he shouldn't forget for even a moment—as if he could.

Keelock slipped, one boot skidding in a wash of mud, sending him stumbling. He fell forward heavily, his hands clawing for purchase, digging into the muck. He clung for a moment, catching his breath, feeling the mud beneath his fingernails. He began moving again, not allowing himself to speculate on what he would find at the top. He scrambled over a rim of jagged stone and found himself on a relatively flat area, partially shielded from the wind and rain. He stood breathing deeply of the cold, damp mountain air, letting the rain wash filth from his palms. He looked down, realizing how far he'd climbed and remembering the conversation with the old man before they parted ways.

"Better tell me what you know, Garrity. And as fast as you can."

Garrity, breathing hard as the shock and pain finally took hold, had shaken his head and answered, "All I know is them kids is—"

"Missing. I know. Tell me about this man."

"What's to tell?" Garrity had shrugged.

When he spoke again, his head tilted towards the mountain's peak, his voice flat and uncertain. "Thought he was just some hombre smoked too much loco weed. He hung around the Capstone for a day or so, makin' eyes at Miss Mason and talkin' nonsense—talkin' about coyotes and crows. He said he had a job to do, and that makin' the 'Key Lock Man' look like a fool was the only way to get even."

Garrity froze then, his eyes going wide. Keelock had winced inwardly at what it did to Garrity's ruined socket.

"By God," Garrity gasped, voice dry with realization. "That's you. It's you, isn't it, you son of a—"

"Skip it," Keelock told him, unwilling to go another round of that kind of talk again. "You come up here to find those kids?"

"Bet your ass," Garrity had replied, pride in his voice. "Me and Mayhan, the big fella from the Capstone, one who slugged you, we made a guess where them runaway cattle was headed and took a shortcut out here. Had a feelin', you could say. Say, I wonder where he's got to—"

"Don't worry about Mayhan," Keelock had said, his voice colder than he intended. "You wanna save those kids, Garrity, you get back to town. Bring wagons, buckboards—whatever you can find and as many as you can find. You'll need 'em when this is all over."

Garrity bristled. "Why the hell should I listen to a thing you say, Keelock? Seems to me you're the one this fella's after, so—"

Keelock was on Garrity then, his revolver digging into the soft underside of the old man's sagging chin. He was fed up with every damned thing, with nooses and coyotes and violence and hatred—and now back-talk, as if Garrity was an unruly child. He had a belly full of it from the old man already and frustration and anger can only be kept in check so long.

"You'll listen," Keelock said quietly, "'cause I'm the one this fella wants, like you said. And I'm the one got plucked from the grave to do what needs be done."

Keelock left the old man behind, repeating his instructions about the wagons, then climbed for what seemed an eternity. The rain and wind warred over him—one fighting him every step of the way, turning dirt to clinging mud and slicking every surface, while the other seemed to push him from behind with an eager hand, as if it wanted to see for itself what this was all about.

Finally, he reached the rim. The wind was fierce now, but that wasn't what gave him pause.

Atop the mountain, the world changed. Rain fell everywhere but here—he could actually see the separation, where the rain simply stopped, like a liquid curtain keeping out prying eyes. He let himself marvel at the strangeness a moment before turning towards the heart of it all.

The black mountain's summit held a shallow bowl cut into its crown, as if scooped out by a giant's trowel. In its center stood a lone figure, distant and small, dwarfed by its surroundings, but plainly visible. The mountain slope had been rocky, covered in broken shale, tough clinging grasses and stunted trees the only growing things. But here, in this hidden place, the ground was thick with black cacti of no species Keelock had ever seen. They were grotesque giants thirty to forty feet tall, clawing at the sky like skeletal hands, their thorns long as sabers and looking just as hard and sharp as any man-made blade.

Keelock moved slowly along the rim, eyes on the unmoving figure in the distance. He was glad to be out of the rain, but the wind still howled, chilling him to the bone—at least he told himself it was only the wind sending shivers through him.

He walked scarcely moments before coming across a set of stairs, carved into the stone of the mountain, descending into the hollow below. He breathed deeply through his nose and slipped the rawhide thong from his holster as he moved down the stairs, grateful at least for solid footing beneath his feet. As he moved, his breath came harder. The air was thinner here, and seemed to catch in the back of his throat. Every breath tasted of copper and was nauseatingly sweet, like rotted fruit soured in the sun.

But he kept on, finding the bottom and moving through a forest of wrong-shaped cactuses. A weird light came from nowhere, illuminating his way. He realized that it was the plants themselves: their spines glowed silvery-blue, as if catching light from a moon that wasn't there.

He considered the cactuses as he walked: they rose like dancers frozen in the middle of some strange routine, their limbs tangled, spines spiraling outward like veins. No two looked the same—some were tall and narrow, others bulged as if bloated, ready to split open. He had the idea that there were things inside of those bloated cactuses, just waiting to claw themselves free from within, and gave them a wide berth.

Down in the hollow, the wind had disappeared and the crunch of fine gravel beneath his feet was the only sound. But that sound was too loud, as if he were twenty feet tall and weighed a thousand pounds, echoing back at him in rhythms that didn't match his steps, despite there being nothing to throw echoes.

And always there were the shadows, writhing at the edge of his vision, retreating when he turned to face them, but never actually gone, dogging his heels stalking beasts.

Lulled by the strange light and sounds, Keelock had fallen into a kind of trance, but a wet rustling sound broke it. He turned, revolver rising, his breath trapped in his chest like a cornered animal.

Two figures watched him from the dark. Two of the goblin-things that had attacked at the base of the mountain. In the cactuses' light, he could see them plainly. One of them wore a faded red bow in the scraps of hair dangling from its scalp, and a tattered dress hung off its twisted limbs like the memory of another life. Its body was warped and wrong, but its face had not yet begun to change and he could see the child within.

Keelock held the weapon steady, lip curled, pity

and revulsion chasing each other inside of his chest.

"Jesus…" he whispered.

The pair watched him, eyes huge and staring, unmoving and silent, as if they were more afraid of him than he of them.

"Poor devils." Keelock holstered the weapon and kept moving. There was only one thing he could do for them.

A clearing opened ahead of him, a ring of the black, thorned giants standing like sentinels. At its center was a shadow, the single figure that Keelock had seen from atop the lip of the hollow.

Keelock stepped into the ring. A black shape cut through the air only feet above his head, making keening noises that lashed all around. He ducked, one hand going to his holster, the other to his hat. "Christ!"

From across the clearing came a soft chuckle. "He's not here, boy—only me!"

Lightning rent the sky, overpowering the cactuses' glow. In the sudden brightness, Keelock saw him: Jay Cooley.

It was Cooley… but changed.

Half of him was blackened, charred from head to toe, like a man who'd walked through fire and come out grinning. Keelock again saw flashes—his memory? No. Cooley's—of the burned church. Screams. Fire. Ash and ruin.

"Cooley," he whispered.

"Surprised?" Cooley asked, grinning through cracked skin.

Keelock shook his head. "Should be, but somehow I'm not."

He gestured vaguely at the mad world around them. "You do all this, Jay?"

"Who, me?" Cooley said. "Nah. Call it a favor from a friend.""

Behind Cooley, the bird landed on the lower arm

of a cactus. Keelock saw it clearly for the first time: a crow, massive, blacker than the night, with a wicked intelligence in its dark, shining eyes.

Keelock jerked his chin at it. "You call that thing a friend?"

"Why not?" Cooley said, teeth flashing. "I was burnin' in hell for what I did durin' the war—that blasted church—and he pulled me free. What's more, he's givin' me what I wanted—" He stepped forward, the grin turning savage. "Another chance at you."

Keelock sneered. "You had your chance, and you played it dirty—and you still lost."

Cooley snarled, "That's a damned lie! I was outta position, if we'd'a been—"

"What about the kids?"

Keelock and Cooley stood at opposite edges of the clearing. As they spoke, goblin-things had crept into view, peeking from behind the twisted, towering plants in ones and twos. Some were only creatures, all fangs and claws and jet-black eyes. But some, like the one with the tattered dress and faded bow, still bore signs of humanity. It wrenched Keelock like nothing ever had.

"You want that, too, Jay?" he asked.

"I didn't know!" Cooley shouted. "But it don't matter! What do I care about kids? This ain't my world anymore, Keelock, nor yours neither!"

"You really hate me that much?" Keelock asked, voice rough and low. "What did I ever do to you?"

Cooley's fists clenched. His voice dropped.

"You stupid bastard… you don't even remember me, do you? Not before I started that talk of horse-thievin'." Cooley bared his teeth like an animal. "But you remember Bella, I reckon."

Images leapt through Keelock's mind, brighter and faster than the lightning above them.

Cattle drives. Whiskey in tin cups. A day or two in town—and a dancehall girl, Bella, laughing in Keelock's arms as they whirled across the dance floor to honky-tonk piano.

He remembered Cooley vaguely now—just another trailhand blowing his pay in the dancehall, Keelock had thought. But next morning, Bella turned up dead in an alley, bright-colored dress stained dark red with dried blood.

"That was you?" Keelock asked, soft and deadly.

Cooley's face twisted. "You took her from me. I took her from you. Only it didn't work like I thought. I didn't feel no better. Just made me hate you more."

Keelock's voice roughened, hatred rising in him to match Cooley's. "God Almighty, Cooley… all that blatherskite about horse-theft was just a smokescreen, tryin' to get me to draw on you?"

Cooley grinned thinly. "It worked, didn't it?"

Keelock's hand went to his gun. "And it'll work again—"

A voice, calm and inhuman, interrupted. "One moment, gentlemen."

Both men froze.

A coyote stood at the side of the clearing. "You might as well join us too—"

The bird moved. As it did, it shrank, settling beside the coyote like a shadow.

"—Crow."

Keelock's gun was up in an instant. "You been with me all along, I suppose?"

"Not at all," Coyote said, his trickster's mask smiling, pleased like everything was going exactly to plan. "I prefer not to interfere, unlike some." He nodded toward the crow, a strange gesture from the canine form.

The bird shifted again, its body growing, stretching. Wings became arms and the body a man's, but the head was still a crow's, feathered and beaked, the eyes piercing.

"You play your way," the bird-man said, "I play mine."

Keelock's voice cracked with rage. "Play? This is a

game to you?"

"Don't sound so surprised, Mr. Keelock," Coyote said, going through its own transformation, reshaping itself into a man with a coyote's head and a coyote's sly doggy grin. "Eternity is a very long time and life can be so very boring."

Keelock turned to Cooley. "You knew?"

Cooley barely shook his head. "Didn't care."

Keelock pointed toward the children-things, the hollowed-out remnants creeping around the periphery of the clearing, as if sensing that their fate was being decided. "Why me? Why Cooley? Why them?"

Crow's voice was like fingernails on bark. "Coyote and Crow—mediators between life and death…"

Coyote joined in: "Keelock and Cooley—one dying, one dead. What better—"

A bullet screamed past Coyote.

"—game pieces could we ask for?"

Keelock's smoking gun drooped. "Those kids ain't pieces in no game."

Coyote shrugged. "Fair enough. Call it what you will, but prove me the winner of this game and I'll gladly put everything aright as if it never happened."

Another shot blazed from Keelock's gun, the barrel's etchings flaring brightly. A hole appeared in Coyote's ear. He didn't even flinch.

"Nice try, Mr. Keelock," he said cheerfully. "But no dice. You couldn't harm me if you lived a thousand years."

Another shot screamed—over Keelock's head.

"Enough talk!" Cooley snarled. "Put your gun up or die where you stand!"

Keelock didn't hesitate. "Fine. Have it your way!"

Both men fired, the gunshots echoing together, overlapping.

Keelock cried out, staggering, blood blooming from his hip.

Cooley reeled, a gaping wound burning in his chest.

He looked stunned, shocked, as if he had never felt pain before.

Keelock exhaled, relief flooding him. "That's that then…"

Cooley's laughter was a ragged breath rising from his own grave. "Oh, you think so?" He smiled, his eyes coin-bright with madness. "Remember what they said? One dying. One dead."

"Shit!" Keelock dove as Cooley opened fire, wild and erratic. Keelock rolled to a sitting position and answered, fanning the revolver as fast as it would fire.

Bullets roared in all directions. The goblin-things scattered into the forest of cactuses, their chittering scarcely heard over the blare of gunfire.

Keelock broke the revolver, dumped empty cartridges and fed fresh ones into the cylinder. He snapped the gun closed again before noticing it—silence.

Peeking from cover, a cactus riddled with holes, he saw Cooley, still standing, but wobbling back and forth like a worn-out pendulum.

"I don't… don't un'erstand…" Cooley mumbled, his eyes confused, voice trembling.

Coyote crouched on a cactus limb above Keelock, pointing toward something beyond Cooley.

"Then have a look for yourselves. I never said how the game was to be won… though I gave you a very fair clue."

Across the clearing, Crow stood utterly still. A single bullet-hole showed in the center of its skull.

Keelock looked to his revolver. "One of my strays…?"

The silvered weapon began to glow, pulsing in time with the pendant against Keelock's chest. The glow steadily grew, intensifying until the light became blinding.

Keelock was forced to shield his eyes, but through parted fingers he saw Crow's body hovering in the air, limbs limp and hanging, as if he were a puppet held by a single string. As Keelock watched, fissures formed in Crow's body, growing bright enough to rival the weapon's brilliance until it ruptured, incandescent light bursting from within, sending particles soundlessly blasting in all directions.

"Good game, Mr. Keelock..." came Coyote's voice from somewhere far away. "Very good indeed."

And then Keelock knew only white—purer than driven snow, purer than the sun at high noon. Blinding, warming, wholesome. When it faded, the air settled slowly, like the mountain had exhaled centuries of dust in one dying breath. The storm had passed—there was no thunder, no rain—replaced by the gentle fall of ash and an overpowering silence.

Keelock coughed and spat, clearing ash and dust from his throat, and rolled onto his side. The revolver lay next to him, still warm. Its silver barrel was scorched black now, cracked like bones in a campfire, and the metal was actually smoking. Useless now, but it served its purpose.

Across the clearing, Jay Cooley slumped at the foot of a cactus, unmoving. Dead for real this time, Keelock hoped.

The eastern sky was a gray glow, signaling the coming dawn. Keelock dragged himself upright, his hip screaming pained fury at him, leaking blood with each movement. It wasn't just his hip, either—he hurt all over, but he was alive.

Limping across the clearing, he realized that the mountain was no longer twisted. The hollow was a strange feature, but only that, and the cactuses had withered, little more than dried husks, as if some unholy energy had been leeched from them. Even the black color was gone, replaced by the brown of a malnourished plant. They were normal cactuses now—dying, but natural.

And the children...

The children came creeping closer from every direction, ragged and confused and scared, but human—and whole.

A little girl dressed in rags, with a faded bow in her hair, peeked out from behind a rock. "Are… are they all gone?" she asked in a tiny voice, as if unsure she really wanted Keelock to hear her.

Keelock looked skyward, towards the growing dawn, then back to the girl. "I reckon it's over."

She hesitated then came from behind the rock. "Can you take us home, mister? It's cold and I'm awful hungry."

Keelock's throat caught and his eyes began to burn and mist. "Yeah, sweetheart."

Dozens of children began to cluster around him, of all shades and all ages from tykes barely walking to a girl eleven or twelve. He held out a hand towards the nearest, a girl of maybe eight, wearing sackcloth. "Let's all go home." She hesitated, looking from Keelock's face to his outstretched hand and then slowly, as if afraid of being hurt but wanting to believe, reached out and grabbed hold. Her fingers trembled but held firmly.

He turned for one last look at Cooley. Before his eyes, the blacked half of Cooley's body spread until not a scrap of unblemished skin showed. The corpse began to smolder, burning rapidly into nothing but ashes. The wind picked up, scattering what was left of Jay Cooley.

"Thank God," Keelock said aloud, unsure of which god he meant, but finally certain the nightmare was over.

Keelock led the children up the stone steps to the rim, and at the top spotted a scatter of wagons, still distant but approaching the base of the mountain. He let out a sound of relief and then allowed himself a small smile. Garrity had done what he was told, probably for the first time in his life.

As Keelock watched the wagons creep closer, a gust of wind swept past. A single crow feather spun through the air, dancing around Keelock as if taunting him. He caught it and, expressionless, tucked the feather inside of his shirt, alongside Coyote's pendant. Then he turned and limped down the mountain with the children in tow.

End

BONUS STORIES

The Right to Hang

(Originally Published October 2021 in On the Premises #38)

Pa squinted at the sun, just dipping behind the hills to the west, one hand shielding his eyes. "'Bout supper-time." Hoe slung over his shoulder, he turned to me. "Hungry, Al?"

"Sure am," I said.

Pa nodded and began walking, his heavy brogans kicking up little puffs of dust on the path between rows of corn sprouts. He was like that: nothing to say unless he really had something to tell you. Imitating him, I put my own hoe on my shoulder and followed.

Halfway between field and house, we stowed the tools in the shed, then Pa pulled up a bucket of water from the well. It tasted sulphury, but it was always cool and that was more important to me after a hot day's work. Pa and me each had a drink, then he dumped what was left over my head, sending a shiver down my spine and making me laugh with pure joy. The tight little smile Pa showed me was about all the emotion I ever saw from him, but I knew he was happy, too. A spread of your own and a son to carry on your name was everything a man could ask for, he once told me.

Pa replaced the bucket then, quiet as ever, headed towards the house. As we reached the low fence that surrounded it, a chorus of squawks and little chirrups greeted us. He ignored the scrawny rooster and six little hens who crowded around his feet, begging for their supper, and continued to the door of the house.

I stopped in the yard, though, and called after him, "Chickens are hungry, Pa."

Without a glance at me or the birds, he answered, "Reckon," and veered off towards the henhouse for the sack of cornmeal, hanging in its rafters.

I stood and watched for a moment, enjoying the happy sounds of the birds as they scrambled and pecked for the meal my father gave 'em, and when he went to put away the sack, I pushed open the door to the house and went inside.

I saw the stranger then.

He was nobody I knew from neighboring homesteads or that I ever saw in town. Finding him in the house brought my heart up into my throat. A twelve-year-old boy may like to think he's about growed, but when something like this comes along, he's a kid again lickety-split.

The man stood, silent and staring, his eyes wide in his unshaven face and a handful of dried apples clutched to his chest. He was narrow-hipped and wide-shouldered, but wasn't a very big man, not much taller than me, even if he was probably fifteen or twenty years older. Pa was about six feet, and this stranger maybe would have come to his shoulder. The man was dressed like a cowpuncher, but his Levis were so filthy they were more dirty brown than blue, with holes worn in the knees and a long, thin tear high on his left thigh, crusted with dried blood. He had no hat and wore no gun-belt, so I knew something was wrong; I never before saw a 'puncher without either.

"Where'd you come from?" Pa's voice boomed

behind me.

The stranger hesitated, looking like he wanted to run. Our house was a soddy, though, with only a single door and a pair of small windows on either side of it. With us between him and the door, there was nowhere for him to go.

The small, dirty man looked from Pa to me. Turning his eyes to the floor, he said tiredly, "Narrow Flats."

Narrow Flats was the nearest town, less'n eight miles away, but I didn't see no horse and it was a ways to walk in a horseman's high-heeled boots.

Pa thought for a moment then said, "Looks like you come the roundabout way."

The stranger smiled weakly. "Reckon so. Don't know this country too good. Guess I got turned around. I saw your place and thought maybe I could get some grub. Nobody was home and…"

"And so you thought you'd steal yourself something?" For the first time in years, there was anger in Pa's voice.

"No, no! I just wanted something to eat, I swear—"

"Look here, mister." My father's voice grew hard in a way I'd never heard. "You came into my house without invitation, looking like you've been crawling through mudholes and over bobwire, so don't hand me no guff. You're running from something, so just tell me about it and then I'll decide what to do with you."

Behind the dirt and the tangle of whiskers, the stranger's face went pale. It was plain he wanted to just run away, but unless Pa let him, there was no way he could. After a moment, he seemed to sag in on himself like an empty sack leaned against a wall. "All right."

Pa gestured towards the table in the center of the room. "Sit down. Let's be civilized about this, at least." He was a good man, and a kind one, even at such a time.

Setting the dried apples on the table, the stranger pulled out a chair, gratitude on his face now. "Obliged."

Pa wasted no time. "What's your name?"

"Lester McCray."

He said it like he expected us to recognize the name, but it meant nothing to me and I could tell it didn't to Pa, neither.

McCray added, "Thought you'da heard of me." Pa said nothing, just stared at the other man. McCray lowered his eyes to the table. "I've been in the pokey over in Narrow Flats the last few days."

"How come you're here now, then?" Pa wanted to know.

McCray took a deep breath. "Folks were getting riled up, said they weren't gonna wait for no trial when they could just have themselves a necktie social and save trouble all around."

"What folks?"

"Whole damned town!" McCray cried. "I heard 'em talkin' all day yesterday, outside the jail, 'bout the circuit judge takin' too long to show up and there bein' no point anyway when they knew I was guilty. The marshal was aimin' to take me to the county seat and stick me in the sheriff's jail soon as it got dark enough to sneak me out, but I didn't trust him. There was something in his eyes when he looked at me…" He shook his head.

"So when he pulled me from the cell last night, I saw my chance, got in a lucky punch and lit a shuck. I ran most'a the night and hid all day in that stand of trees yonder from your place." McCray waved a hand. "I wanted to keep on goin', but I had to eat somethin' and then I saw your house and…" He trailed off again.

Pa stared at McCray a long time, digesting what the other man said, I guessed – maybe trying to decide if McCray was telling the truth or not. Finally, Pa asked, "What did you do to rile folks so bad?"

Lester McCray waited plenty long before answering

and when he did, he seemed to be choosin' his words real careful. "They say I killed a girl."

The room was awful still all of a sudden, as if everything, even our heartbeats, had stopped. I stood next to the table, trying to keep all my attention on both men at once, wondering what would come next, scarcely daring to breath for all the tension. Images flashed through my mind, of Pa overpowering McCray, tying him up, throwing him in the bed of the wagon and bringing him back to town, being treated like a hero by all the neighbors.

Or maybe that was too much trouble. Maybe Pa should just take down the scattergun over the hearth and put an end to McCray himself. If McCray really was a woman-killer, that was the least he deserved.

"Did you?" Pa asked, real quiet.

McCray's face scrunched up. "What difference does it make? Them folks already made up their minds."

"It ain't up to them, just like it ain't up to me," Pa answered. "That's what it matters. We got laws for a reason." He sighed and leaned back in the chair. He cast a glance at me before turning back to McCray. "Fact remains, though, that whether you did anything else, you broke jail and I got to turn you in."

"To that mob?" McCray got pale all over again.

"No." Pa shook his head. "I believe in the law and every man's got a right to a fair trial. If you can't trust the marshal, I'll turn you over to the sheriff." He indicated me with his head. "I can send Al up to the county jail with a note for Sheriff McLaughlin." Something sang in my chest when he said that. I was never trusted with anything so important before.

Relief came into McCray's eyes. "That's something, anyway."

"I will see you into the law's hands, though, McCray. Don't believe for an instant I won't." Without looking at me, he added, "Al, get the scattergun. Make sure it's loaded."

"Yes, sir!" I snapped. Pa spoke more words in the last few minutes than he did all together in the past week and the importance of what was happening hung heavy in the air all around us. I moved to the hearth and lifted the gun down. From the cabinet by Pa's bunk, I took out the box of shotgun cartridges, broke open the gun and fitted a cartridge into each barrel.

That's when I saw them.

I was so focused on first the gun, then loading it, that I didn't notice the men outside, coming from the direction of the woods, until they were halfway across our fields.

"Pa…" I said.

He must have heard something in my voice, because he left his chair and joined me by the window. He only looked for a moment before moving away from it again. To McCray, he said, "Guess they tracked you."

"What're you gonna do, Pa?" I asked, my voice high-pitched with fear. Ordinarily, I'd be embarrassed by such a thing, but I didn't even notice then.

Both McCray and I watched pa as he worked it over in his mind. I kept stealing glances outside. The men out there weren't hurrying, but they were closer each time I looked, and they were making straight for the house.

"I won't let them take you, Mr. McCray," Pa finally said.

My throat thick, I asked, "You gonna fight all those fellers, Pa?"

Pa looked at me. "I won't fight any man unless he forces me." He indicated the shotgun with his chin. "Hold onto that, Al. Guard McCray. They won't take him if we can help it, but don't you let him loose, either."

I nodded. My mouth was suddenly too dry for words. I looked at McCray, then quickly turned my eyes away again. I was terrified, but almighty proud, too. Pa was trusting me just the same as he would trust a full-growed man.

Pa looked to the stranger. "You get all that, McCray? Just keep quiet and stay put. I'll go out there and when those fellers ask, I'll tell them I haven't seen anything, don't know anything, never heard of you." McCray's head bobbed up and down.

Pa went to the window. The men were past the fields now, almost to the house. He turned to me. "No man deserves hangin' without a trial, Al. Those folks out there are mostly good, but they're scared and angry and that can make 'em lose their sense. It ain't up to them or us to judge anybody. That's why laws and courts exist." His eyes shifted to McCray. "Laws protect all of us, guilty or innocent. You understand me?"

I swallowed hard, my head nodding.

Pa nodded back, turned and went out the door.

I wedged myself into a corner where I could see through the nearest window, hoping I couldn't be seen from outside. With the shotgun, I gestured to McCray and he got the message, cramming himself into the opposite corner, in back of the house, where nobody could see him. The way we were positioned, I could cover both the door and McCray with the shotgun without moving too much. My heart was beating so hard, though, and my hands were so slippery with sweat, I didn't know if I'd actually be able to was it necessary.

Through the corner of the window, I saw Pa tromp across the dusty dooryard, scattering chickens. He met the possemen at the fence surrounding the house, Pa inside and the other men out. He lifted a hand and his mouth moved, but I couldn't hear the words. One of the men moved out of the group, a big, rawboned man I recognized from around town, named Stevens. He held a Winchester in both hands and there was a sixgun strapped to his hip. His eyes were shaded by a dusty-black planter's hat, but his mouth worked fast and I could tell he was angry.

Stevens and Pa talked for a minute or so and then, from somewhere in the mass of men, a voice called, "The hell we'll take him back! We'll hang him from the nearest tree!" One of the small panes was missing from the window and I could hear the words, but didn't know who of the ten or twelve men out there said 'em.

"Then I'm glad he ain't here!" my father shouted back.

Stevens stepped forward, brandishing his rifle, pushing his way through the gate in the fence. He was close enough and loud enough that I could clearly hear him say, "Sticking up for McCray, are you, Sloan?"

"Sticking up for the law," Pa answered. "Only the courts got the right to hang a man."

"You a law-yer now, Sloan?" Stevens jeered. There was a chuckle from somewhere in the posse, but it sounded weak and tired.

"He's guilty!" someone shouted. "Old man Drake found McCray's hat in his yard and two other folks say they saw him leaving the place."

"Let them tell it to the judge," Pa said.

There was a kind of growl from Stevens. "We come to ask you to join us in the search, Sloan, but I got a feeling we won't be looking much longer."

"I wouldn't join a lynch mob no matter how nice you asked, Stevens."

The big man opened his mouth to reply, but a rail-thin fellow dressed like a townsman yelped, "Hey! Ain't that blood?" his finger outstretched.

As one, every man turned to the dark stain on the top bar of the fence, by the gate. Neither me or Pa noticed before, but pointed out, it was plain.

"Reckon it might be," Pa said. "I killed a chicken for supper."

"Is that right?" Stevens asked.

The thin man who spotted the blood swiveled his head towards the others. "Was McCray hurt anywhere?"

"Found scraps of denim on some bobwire a ways back," someone answered.

"How about it, Sloan?" Stevens snarled. "Got a supper guest?"

"Ain't seen this McCray," Pa said, matter-of-factly.

"Then you won't mind if we take us a quick looksee inside." Stevens made to push past Pa.

I turned towards McCray. Even half-hidden in the shadows at the back of the room, he looked scared and frail. He pressed his back so hard against the wall, it seemed like he was trying to burrow right inside it.

"You stay out of my house, Isaac Stevens." Pa said it real loud, like he was warning all the men, not just Stevens.

"A look won't hurt if you got nothing to hide." Stevens shoved Pa away as two other men leapt the fence to restrain him.

As the possemen grabbed pa, he cried, "Al, watch out!"

I had no time for deciding what to do. The door swung open and a huge shape, black against the growing night outside, filled it. Stevens stepped inside, the Winchester rifle leading him. He paused, letting his eyes grow accustomed to the darkness. I could have shot him down in that moment, but my heart was racing and I was too scared to lift the gun. I was so prideful when Pa needed my help that I forgot for a few minutes that I was still just a twelve-year-old boy.

"Put the gun down, kid," Stevens ordered and I knew his eyes were adjusted because he was pointing the Winchester right at me.

I tried again to lift the scattergun, but my arms wouldn't obey. I heard someone shout, "Don't take another step or I'll blast you!" It was a moment before I recognized my own voice.

"Fine. I can shoot from here," Stevens said and brought the rifle in line with where McCray huddled in the corner of the room.

I was scared so bad I thought I might pee myself, but Pa trusted me and that meant a lot. Somehow, I found the strength to bring the shotgun up and before I knew it, the right barrel was belching fire and the Winchester was spinning out of Stevens's hands.

"Yooowch!" he bellowed.

Faces appeared at the windows and Stevens, his own face full of rage, clutching his right hand to his chest, shouted, "Get Sloan in here!"

Nobody moved. Stevens roared again, sounding like a wounded bull, and then many hands pushed my father forward, through the door, to stumble into the house. Stevens was breathing heavily as he wrapped his right arm around Pa's throat and with his left hand, pressed the barrel of his sixgun to Pa's head. "Tell your boy to put the gun down, Sloan."

Pa looked at me and I think he was trying to decide how scared I was, how much I understood of what was going on, and whether he could ask any more of me. I did my best to look brave, and slowly, he said, "Al, you just stay where you are. Keep hold of that gun and you shoot down any man who takes a step towards Mr. McCray."

That made Stevens even madder. Even in the worsening darkness, I could see his eyes get bigger and wider, and his jaw clenched in fury. He let go of Pa's neck and nudged him with his shoulder, making Pa stumble again, then smashed him in the side of the head with the butt of his revolver. Pa might have fallen, but suddenly two other men were inside the house to grab and hold him up.

It happened fast and my anger rose just as quickly, burning away the fear. I raised the scattergun to my shoulder, aiming at Stevens. I didn't fire, though; I didn't dare. Pa would be caught in the pellets' spray. My eyes strained, searching through the gloom for the rifle Stevens dropped, wishing I had it instead of the shotgun. If I had a rifle, I could have picked off Stevens and the men holding Pa without touching a hair on his head.

"What's the matter, boy?" Stevens said the last word like it was something dirty. "Don't like seeing your Pa hurt, huh?"

My chest clenched and my finger tightened against the trigger. My mind raced. I didn't know what to do. My eyes bounced from Pa to Stevens to McCray hoping someone, anyone, would give me the answer. McCray, too, was waiting, crouched down, looking less and less like a man and more like a scared, hunted animal.

Stevens was the first to decide. His long, beefy arm shot out, latching onto Pa's collar, ignoring the pain it must have caused his injured hand, and pulled him close. He swung Pa around like a ragdoll then pressed the sixgun against the back of Pa's head. I still had Stevens covered with the shotgun, but now Pa was between me and the big, hateful man. "Put the gun down, boy. Is McCray's life worth your pa's?"

"What do I do, pa?" I cried, feeling hot tears rolling down my cheeks. I hadn't cried in almost three years, not since ma passed, but the fear and the anger were just too much.

"You shoot if you have to, Al," Pa said, calmer than I could have imagined.

Shoot Pa? To save a woman-killer like Lester McCray? I couldn't believe my ears. And even if I did, how would that save the man? Even if I killed Stevens, there were a dozen others to take his place.

Stevens must have read my mind because a grin spread across his face. He pushed Pa forward, putting the two of them squarely in front of me, using Pa as a shield. "You don't want to shoot your Pa, boy. McCray ain't worth it. Put the gun down." When I didn't, he repeated himself, shouting, "Put the gun down!"

"Do what I told you, Al!" Pa yelled.

The sights at the end of the gun-barrels wobbled and it was getting hard to see through the mist in my eyes. Pa struggled, but couldn't break Stevens's grip, not with that sixgun at his head. Others crowded into the house behind Stevens, eager to get in on the "justice" they planned to dish out.

For an instant, my eyes cleared and I saw Pa looking squarely at me. He stopped struggling against Stevens, then his chin dipped the slightest bit, and I knew that it was a signal. With every ounce of willpower in my body, I steadied the scattergun and fired.

A lot of things happened all at once. Men screamed – more than just Stevens and Pa. Lead pellets zinged around the room, burying themselves in wood and flesh. The possemen were pushing and shoving, falling over each other, trying to get out through the narrow doorway and into the safety of the night.

Pa and Stevens were separated now. Stevens was on the floor, clutching a ruined knee, wailing and sobbing. Pa was leaning against the overturned table, inspecting the bloody gash in his denims where the spray of pellets tore through the pants and the meat of his leg.

McCray, ghostly white, eyes huge and staring, collapsed to the floor, pulled his knees up to his chest and put his head on top of them.

*

Solemnly, the circuit judge's deep voice intoned, "For the murder of Sadie Drake, I sentence the accused, Lester McCray, to hang by the neck until dead." With a crash like thunder, his wooden gavel fell on the table, ringing across the temporary courtroom.

A pleased-sounding murmur went through the folk assembled in the Longhorn Saloon. I tried not to look at Lester McCray. I didn't want to know what was on his face.

My father, sitting against the wall by the door, levered himself to his feet with the aid of the crutch Doc Feeny loaned him days earlier. "Let's go, Al," he told me and turned towards the street.

People streamed around us, headed towards the square where the gallows, built the night before, stood. There was a carnival atmosphere, like when the rodeo was thrown a year ago to celebrate the five-year anniversary of

Narrow Flats's founding. None of that happiness touched either Pa or me.

When we reached the buckboard, I made to help Pa up onto the seat. He put his hand on my shoulder, but instead of propelling himself upwards, he looked straight into my eyes and said, "It was always going to end like this, Al, and I don't say it's right, but this way, it's legal at least. Do you understand why that's important?"

I wasn't sure if I did, but I just nodded. I didn't think I could handle any more lessons. Not on this subject, not for a while. I helped Pa up onto the bench and we set off for home. Neither one of us said a word all the rest of the day.

End

The Home Place

(Originally published March 2020 as a Full Speed Single)

The sun was high overhead as I loosed the last of the three, small cayuses into the pole corral just down the hill from my family's cabin. The largest of them, still less than fourteen hands, bucked wildly and snorted fury at me, his jailer. He ignored the two still half-wild horses already in the corral, as well as his fellows I'd brought in with him. I was his enemy and he wouldn't let me forget it.

I shook my head at him. "Sorry, fella, but you know how it is."

Well, he probably didn't at that, but I did and lately, it was not good at all.

We—my wife, Linda Jane, our five-year-old son Jim, Jr and I—had come into the Nation, the Indian Territory, with a plan: to round up wild horses, break them, breed them, and sell the resulting herds to all the folks coming in for land grants now that the Nation was being opened up to homesteaders. I knew horses, having worked on a Morgan ranch in Kentucky most of my life, and a trip out west in my youth showed me both wild herds and possibilities. Every dollar we had went into moving our small family west, and bringing along a good, solid Morgan stud to start our own ranch.

It was a good plan, but nobody told it to the Indians and they had plans of their own. We made it to the Nation, staked our claim, built us a cabin, a lean-to barn and a corral, and no sooner had I left on my first trip to round up wild ponies when a raiding band of some tribe or another—either Comanches or Kiowas, it must have been, though I never did figure which—come up on the ranch, stole that Morgan horse, the four mules who pulled our wagon west, and would have made off with Linda Jane's milk cow, too, if she hadn't the foresight to pull it right into the cabin and the sand to hold them braves off with my old Colt's revolving shotgun.

When I come back home, I was right proud of her, if grieved by the loss of those animals, and worse grieved by her demand that we give up all this foolishness, as she called it, and head on back 'home.' "This is home," I told her, reminding her we had no way of going back to Kentucky without money or even horses beyond my saddle-horse and the four, still-wild Mustangs I caught on that first trip. She didn't argue, seeing the logic of what I said, and life settled down some, but things were never really quite right after that.

And I had no time to argue anyway; without the stud I spent so much money to obtain, the dream of my own ranch was still possible, but much farther off. I needed to pull together enough wild stock to make my own herd, break them, and sell off enough to either buy me another pedigreed stud horse or live on while I made a go with what I had. And it turned out I wasn't the only one in the country with that same idea, either. Things went pretty good, considering, for a few months, but then I found the herds getting smaller and farther apart. Before long, I learned why: a big operation from up north a ways, called the Lazy D, had exhausted their own territory and come down here to continue their round ups.

They gave me hell, chasing me off grounds where I'd rounded up good stock before, with their sheer numbers and an implied threat of violence that I wasn't prepared to handle.

So I moved further out, into places I'd ignored or going after stock I knew to be of lesser quality, worth less money. What else could I do? I had no way to stop the Lazy D; it was federal land and those horses belonged to nobody but themselves until someone tamed and branded them. I couldn't outwork them, either, not on my lonesome, and I had no money to hire hands. I couldn't even promise anyone a share of the income from the horses, as there was little enough to support my own family, much less someone else's. All I could do was keep my head down, keep my mind on my business, and steer clear of trouble as much as possible.

Months dragged on, the work growing harder and less profitable, the hostility from the competition stronger and more blatant. I no longer dared camp out in the open; too many times, I woke up in the morning to find whatever I'd gathered the day before gone without a trace. The dream of my own ranch, my own herd, wasn't dead, but it sure wasn't healthy, either.

Now, as I approached the cabin, I saw Linda Jane, standing in the doorway of the split-log cabin we built together. The sun was noon-time hot, and there was a warm wind coming out from the drylands, gently rustling the stray strands of hair that escaped from the bun at the back of her head. I waved but Linda Jane just turned on her heel and went inside. I let out a sigh. Things hadn't been the same between us for a long time, but I didn't know what to do short of pulling up stakes and there was just no chance it was going to happen. Running back east was out of the question even if there was a way to do it. It would be admitting defeat and while I was not a proud man, exactly, I also was neither beaten nor a quitter.

I went through the little gate in the fence that surrounded the dooryard garden Linda Jane put in to keep us in fresh vegetables. The leafy greens of the carrot tops and the yellow of the squash looked good against the dark, healthy soil, and the peapods were starting to get fat and heavy. I was proud of her hard work and she should have been able to take pride in it, too, but I knew she didn't. She saw it as nothing more than survival, which it was, but it wasn't only that. It was a sign, a mark she made on this land, the same as I was trying to make mine. I wished that she could see it the way I did.

I washed my hands in the bucket beside the door, knocked the dust off my boots, and went inside. Linda Jane put our luncheon on the table her daddy made us himself as a wedding gift, nearly six years ago. More than once on the way west, I wanted to leave it aside the trail, freeing up space and weight in the wagon, telling her I could make a new one when we arrived. But she wouldn't hear of any such thing and now, I was glad that we kept it. Luxuries were almighty scarce in those days and in that country and it was a thing to take pride in, something solidly connecting us to our past that we could carry on into the future. Maybe someday it would be more than us three sitting around it. The thought of more kids, and even grandkids, growing up on this land of ours was a not so secret pleasure of mine.

The smell of the meal was in the air of the cabin, heavy and hearty and good. Vegetables from the garden, some squaw cabbage I'd gathered while on a hunting trip, and stewed venison from the same. There was no bread or biscuits, but then, there hadn't been flour in almost a week. I hadn't been to town in three times that long, with little to sell and little money to buy anything with. But we got by and I knew we still ate better than did some of the folks back in Kentucky.

Linda Jane was at the wash-basin rinsing dishes. Jim, Jr was seated at the table, waiting patiently for me, his eyes glued to the steaming bowl in front of him. I seated myself, saying, "Sure looks good, Linda Jane. Garden looks good, too. Those carrots'll be ready to pull up before too long."

My wife said only, "You better just eat, Jim. We been waiting on you."

"Not without you. Come on, sit down. I got three ponies this morning, right nearby, hardly six miles out. Strange to find 'em so close, but I ain't complaining. We're due a little luck. It might just keep on, too," I continued. "I saw some tracks I want to follow, least half a dozen in the group. Probably be gone 'til tomorrow, but if it works out, I might could end up with a full dozen cayuses to sell over in town before the end of the week."

She turned, but her eyes would not look at me. There was a slight movement of her shoulders, as if she was shrugging off an unwanted touch. I saw her lips move, but I didn't catch what she said.

"What was that, honey?" I asked.

"It was nothing, Jim."

"C'mon, now, honey. I know you don't like me being gone overnight, but you know I got to—"

"You want to know what I said, Jim Maddern?" Her eyes rose, stabbing across the room at me, a tired kind of anger in them. It was familiar, something that I knew had long simmered inside her, but it was only rarely that she let show.

"Yes, ma'am." I honestly did, though I felt I knew what was coming.

"I said 'what's the use?' What is the use, Jim? No matter how many of those sad little ponies you been bringin' in, you'll never make enough money to keep us alive and build your god da—" Her eyes strayed to Jim, Jr for an instant, then swung back to me. "Gosh darned ranch, much less a breeding herd. What good does it do, selling those scrawny ponies in twos and threes, for – what? Eight dollars apiece? Ten, at most? They ain't good cow ponies, they ain't plow horses; they ain't good for anything. And yet you persist in this… this foolishness!"

It was that word again, that word she knew I hated. The word she used that first time, after the Indian raid. What could I say to it? What could I say in my defense? She wasn't wrong about the facts, only where they led, and I couldn't tell her different, I could only show her. And for that I needed time.

So I said nothing. I just looked at my wife, waiting for whatever came next.

"Mama…" little Jim said in his smallest voice.

Linda Jane turned her gaze to the boy and said, "Eat your food, Jimmy," using the name only she ever called him. To me, low-voiced, she said, "Is this what you want for your son, Jim?" She gestured towards the food, growing cold now. "Eating weeds and wild meat and living on the edge of that god-forsaken desert, while other men steal your livelihood out from under your nose?"

"This is our home," I said, matching her quiet, grave tone.

"Home!" She barked, half-sob, half-laugh, drawing Jim, Jr's startled gaze. "This is no home, Jim Maddern, it's a prison."

The room suddenly grew very still. It was as if we were all holding our breath. Even little Jim, hungry as he must have been, paused with his spoon halfway to his mouth.

The stillness was broken by the sound of horses in the dooryard. It was not the wild ponies in the corral just down the hill – it was the sound of shod hooves stamping the hard-packed dirt and the jingle and clatter of tackle. A moment later came a shout: "Hello, the house!"

I rose from the table and moved to the doorway, pulling aside the bit of lace that Linda Jane had fashioned as a curtain for the little, glassless window set near the top of the door. In the dooryard were three horses and on each sat a man, and I didn't like the look of any of them.

The foremost was a big, sloppy-looking fellow with

sagging jowls, covered in dirty-ginger whiskers. His fist gripped the stock of a Spencer .56 repeater, the big rifle laid across the bow of his saddle. Around his thick waist was buckled a six-gun, and on his buckskin vest, he wore a badge that even from this distance seemed battered and tarnished. Flanking the apparent leader were two other men, each as shifty-looking as the first, and each as well-armed, though unlike the first man's, their long-guns were scabbarded.

My hand went to my own hip, where I carried an old Rogers and Spencer .44 I'd traded for along the trail west. I had a Winchester repeater, too, but it was still in the scabbard on my saddle-horse, out in the lean-to barn, as I planned to go right back out that afternoon. I looked over my shoulder at Linda Jane, who moved behind Jim, Jr, her arms protectively encircling him.

"It's okay," I told them, hoping it was true. We had no close neighbors and very rarely had visitors. My stock wasn't good enough, as Linda Jane reminded me, for anyone to make a trip out here to buy. The only other reasons men such as these might come calling were all things I didn't want to think too much about. Despite that, and the look of these men, it wasn't necessarily true that they meant trouble.

Slowly, I opened the door and stepped out onto the porch, nudging the door closed behind me with the heel of my boot. "Hello, fellas."

"You James Maddern, mister?" the big man with the tarnished star demanded.

I stepped from the porch, into the dooryard. "I'm Jim Maddern. Who's asking, you don't mind?"

"Who's asking?" the other man taunted, looking to either side at his companions. "Who's asking, he says! Forget that, boy," he said, gesturing with that big Spencer. "Wanna tell me where you got those horses over yonder?"

I followed his gaze towards the corral, not sure what he was getting at. "I gathered those cayuses out near Trinity Canyon. That's how I make my living, if it's any business of yours, catching and breaking wild ponies."

The jowly man sneered. "If it's any business of mine? Christ, son, you know you're talking to the sheriff of this here county you're livin' in? And I say bull-hockey on your story. I say those horses were stolen from the Lazy D outfit's camp down by Sagarillo Gap. And I also say if you know what's good for you, you'll tie 'em up into a lead line and get 'em ready for me to take 'em back."

A little bit of ice seeped into my belly, but I tried not to let it show. I hadn't heard of any sheriff in the area. Only law I knew of was Brett Tilson, the sleepy old marshal of Octilloville, the town twelve miles east of us. I knew damned sure I hadn't stolen those horses, though.

A sinking feeling hit me. It had seemed too damned easy to gather those ponies and they were too damned close to home. Barely out of my backyard. I hadn't seen a soul that day either going out to Trinity or coming back home, so how did these fellows know I brought those ponies home? I was being set up.

"Begging your pardon, mister," I said, at last. "But that just ain't true about those horses being Lazy D's. I ain't never stole a thing in my life and I've been here almost a year gathering up wild stock. Ask anyone, including those Lazy D folks. They might not like it, but they know I was here before them and they know that I stick to my business."

"You know, Maddern…" The big, jowly man paused to exchange grins with his friends, one of whom began to titter in a way that wasn't wholesome. "They hang horse thieves in these parts and as sheriff of this here county, I got every right to string you up," he finished.

From the house, Linda Jane's voice called out, "You're a damned liar, mister! My husband's no horse thief and you ain't no sheriff! There ain't even a county to elect a sheriff! Only law outside of town is the U.S. Marshal and you ain't him!"

The fat man turned from me, pointed an angry finger at the house and growled, "You better come out and let me get a look at you as you apologize for that remark, lady. If you ask nice, I'll even let you see this here badge of my office."

My eyes went to the man's chest and sure enough, as I saw before, there was a star there. I could see that it was old, though, tarnished, and one of the six points of the star was broken off. If this man was sheriff of anything, it was a mighty poor place.

"You leave my wife alone, mister! This is between you and me. In fact, I think I'll ask you kindly to leave my property, now that we've said all we're going to."

The big man in the tarnished star looked back over at me, his teeth clenched in anger. I was angry, too, at being called a horse thief and at these unfair odds, but there was still plenty of caution in me. I was facing three armed men and despite wearing a six-gun, I was no shootist or gunfighter.

The men across from me had to know that, too, because the one with the star gestured with his rifle and said, "Any time you take issue with anything I've said, Maddern, you go right ahead and reach for that hog-leg on your hip. Hell, I'd be glad if you did. Save me the trouble of a hanging." The man to left of the "sheriff" chuckled.

The door opened behind me and I risked a glance over my shoulder. Linda Jane stood in the doorway, the Colt's revolving shotgun she'd stood off a band of raiders with leveled at the chest of the man wearing that broken, probably stolen, star. "You wanted me to come out, mister, well, here I am, but it ain't to apologize. I came out to tell you that if you don't get off my land, like my husband asked you, I'll make sure we find a nice quiet corner of it for you to stay in forever. I'll even toss your badge in after you, for whatever comfort it'll bring you."

Her voice was steel and her eyes blazed. The anger that had lived so long in her was full out in the open now and I was glad it wasn't aimed at me. I stepped to one side as quickly and quietly as I could, not wanting to be between my wife and whatever happened next.

"If you turn around now and get right out of my dooryard, mister," Linda Jane continued, something dark and dangerous that I'd never heard before in her voice, "we'll forget this ever happened, as long as I never lay eyes on you again. But if you come back here or I hear of you bothering my husband while he's about his right and legal business, I'll track down that federal marshal myself and ask him the question of whether or not this country has got any sheriff."

The would-be sheriff paled for an instant, then bared his teeth. "You god damned little hussy! I'll show you who's—" He began, bringing up the hand that grasped the stock of his rifle.

He never finished the sentence and never even got that gun in line to fire. Linda Jane's shotgun cut loose with a tremendous roar, sending out a spray of buckshot. That false sheriff's chest became a shredded, bloody mess and he dropped from his horse like he was pole-axed.

I was stunned into silence. I was proud of my wife for thinking quicker than I, for first realizing there could be no sheriff when there wasn't even a county yet, for knowing that it was some sort of trick by the Lazy D outfit trying to run me out of the horse business and maybe kill me in the process. I was proud of her for taking action to defend us, too. But I never thought the trouble between me and the Lazy D would come this. I'd seen men die along the trail, fighting Indians, and once, robbers who thought a train of pilgrims were easy pickings. Living in the west, I expected I'd see it again someday, but I never imagined it would be my own wife doing the shooting. I was a little dazed, but still I was proud of, and glad for, that sand she showed.

I came back to the moment and saw those two shady fellows still ahorse were almighty still, knowing Linda Jane had three more shots in that gun and surely afraid she'd cut loose again. Their boss tried arguing with Linda Jane, but there was no arguing with that shotgun. One rider stared down at the man who lay broken and bleeding in the dust. The other's mouth moved like a fish out of water, eyes wide, gawping at Linda Jane.

I pulled the revolver from my holster and whistled to get their attention. "Pick that man up, get him onto that horse, and ride out of here. You got about one minute before my wife cuts loose again." I glanced at Linda Jane and she gave me a nod in return.

With two guns on them and their "sheriff" dead or dying, those fellows knew their minds. They dismounted, lifted the bulk of the third man onto the back of his horse, tied him in place, and then hightailed it out of the yard, heading north towards the low, distant hills. As they hurried away, I noticed a sideways-tilted "D" on the haunch of the dead man's mount.

We stood in place, listening to the receding sounds of the horses' hooves, watching their dust settle in the distance, making sure they weren't coming back with friends.

After a spell, I put that old Rogers and Spencer back into its holster, took a deep, shuddering breath and turned to Linda Jane. "By god, you sure showed them."

All that time we waited, she stood in the doorway, holding that Colt's rock-steady, a look of grim determination on her face. It was a new world, but she was a very old breed of woman: a wife and mother, defending what was hers, protecting those she loved.

And now, finally, she looked at me, and something hard went out of those eyes while something softer replaced it. Letting the Colt's fall from her fingers to clatter onto the porch, she ran from the doorway, across the yard, throwing her arms around my neck. "Oh Lord, Jim, I was so scared! I don't know what came over me, I just knew… I mean, I just—"

"No, honey," I said, stroking her back, nuzzling the soft brown hair that still smelled faintly of soap. "You knew exactly what you were doing, same as the night you held off those Indians. You were defending your home."

Linda Jane pulled back, looked me in the eyes and, after a moment, said, "I guess you just don't know what's important 'til someone tries to take it away from you."

I smiled and kissed her.

Jim, Jr stuck his head out of the doorway, looking around cautiously, eyes wide as they fell on the splatter of blood in the yard. "Is it done, daddy?" he asked in his baby voice.

"Not quite, son," I told him. To Linda Jane, still in my arms, I said, "I guess I better ride into town, tell Marshal Tilson."

"That's a good idea. He can send for the federal marshal. Maybe now they'll finally do something about that Lazy D crew."

I nodded. "Maybe so. Well," I released my wife, not wanting to, not wanting to leave her, but knowing there was still plenty to do before the day was done. "I better get riding if I want to be back before nightfall."

Linda Jane walked to the porch, scooped our son up her arms and turned back to me. "All right, Jim. Be careful. I'll have supper ready when you get home."

I smiled as I walked towards the barn and my saddle-horse. It was the first time Linda Jane had called this place that – home. And I knew now that it wouldn't be the last.

End

ABOUT THE AUTHOR

Brandon Barrows is the author of a dozen novels, his most recent *Long Before They Die* from Full Speed Publishing. He has also published over one hundred short stories for which he is a four-time Mustang Award finalist for excellence in western fiction and a two-time Derringer Award nominee for excellence in crime and mystery fiction.

Find more at
http://www.brandonbarrowscomics.com

www.ingramcontent.com/pod-product-compliance
Lightning Source LLC
LaVergne TN
LVHW090533110826
845146LV00003B/1075

9798985472578